THE TRUTH ABOUT ME & BOBBY V.

This is it, I thought. This is what being a teenager is all about. I grinned and stole a glance at Flip. He looked just right for the part he was going to play.

Me and Bobby V., I thought happily.

Flip must have sensed me looking at him. He smiled.

"Just you and me, baby, right?" he said.

The moment we pulled into the parking lot was worth all those nights I worried about the lie I'd told. In fact, just watching Diana's face when she saw Flip was worth everything, even the terrible punishment my grandma said would happen to me.

Bantam Sweet Dreams Romances
Ask your bookseller for the books you have missed

P.S. I LOVE YOU by Barbara Conklin
LITTLE SISTER by Yvonne Greene
LAURIE'S SONG by Suzanne Rand
PRINCESS AMY by Melinda Pollowitz
CALIFORNIA GIRL by Janet Quin-Harkin
THE POPULARITY PLAN by Rosemary Vernon
GREEN EYES by Suzanne Rand
THE THOROUGHBRED by Joanna Campbell
COVER GIRL by Yvonne Greene
LOVE MATCH by Janet Quin-Harkin
THE PROBLEM WITH LOVE by Rosemary Vernon
NIGHT OF THE PROM by Debra Spector
THE SUMMER JENNY FELL IN LOVE by Barbara Conklin
DANCE OF LOVE by Jocelyn Saal
THINKING OF YOU by Jeanette Nobile
HOW DO YOU SAY GOODBYE by Margaret Burman
ASK ANNIE by Suzanne Rand
TEN-BOY SUMMER by Janet Quin-Harkin
ALL'S FAIR IN LOVE by Jeanne Andrews
SECRET IDENTITY by Joanna Campbell
FALLING IN LOVE AGAIN by Barbara Conklin
THE TROUBLE WITH CHARLIE by Jaye Ellen
HER SECRET SELF by Rhondi Vilott
IT MUST BE MAGIC by Marian Woodruff
TOO YOUNG FOR LOVE by Gailanne Maravel
TRUSTING HEARTS by Jocelyn Saal
NEVER LOVE A COWBOY by Jesse DuKore
LITTLE WHITE LIES by Lois I. Fisher
CLOSE TO YOU by Debra Spector
DAYDREAMER by Janet Quin-Harkin
DEAR AMANDA by Rosemary Vernon
COUNTRY GIRL by Melinda Pollowitz
FORBIDDEN LOVE by Marian Woodruff
SUMMER DREAMS by Barbara Conklin
PORTRAIT OF LOVE by Jeanette Nobile
RUNNING MATES by Jocelyn Saal
FIRST LOVE by Debra Spector
SECRETS by Anna Aaron
THE TRUTH ABOUT ME & BOBBY V. by Janetta Johns
THE PERFECT MATCH by Marian Woodruff

The Truth About Me & Bobby V.

Janetta Johns

BANTAM BOOKS
TORONTO · NEW YORK · LONDON · SYDNEY

RL 6, IL age 11 and up

THE TRUTH ABOUT ME & BOBBY V.
A Bantam Book / July 1983

Cover photo by Pat Hill

ISBN 0-553-23531-1

Published simultaneously in the United States and Canada

PRINTED IN THE UNITED STATES OF AMERICA

O   0 9 8 7 6 5 4 3 2 1

Chapter One

As usual, my father broke the news to us in the middle of dinner. He always chose mealtimes to break really big news. That was probably because my mother got excited really easily, and he figured that she was calmest when she was chewing. So he would wait until she was in the middle of dessert and looking calm and content before he said, "Guess what, Martha—the mechanic at the auto shop says the car needs a new engine!"

That night we were right in the middle of peach pie—Grandma's homemade peach pie, made with the peaches that grew in her garden, when he said quietly, "Oh, by the way, Martha—I've got some good news. I'm going to be promoted."

My mother looked up, a forkful of pie balanced in her hand. "Promoted, Harry? Why, that's wonderful," she said.

My brother Freddie stopped eating for a good three seconds—a miracle if you have ever seen my brother eat. He normally shovels it in as if every meal could be his last. This news was so startling that he actually put down his fork, exclaiming, "Hey, right on! Dad just got himself a raise!"

"What are you going to be, Dad?" I asked, feeling all warm inside for him. He looked proud and excited, just like I do when I get a good report card.

"You are looking at the new supervisor in charge of shipping and receiving," he said.

"In charge—wow!" I exclaimed.

Mom looked up sharply from her peach pie. "But I thought there was no shipping done from this branch," she said.

"That's right," Dad said. "All the shipping comes out of the head office."

"And where's that?"

"Out in Walnut Park," he said, and he low-red his eyes as Mom frowned.

"Walnut Park?" she asked. "But that's an hour's drive from the city. Think of all that money for gas and the time it will take to get there."

Dad looked up and smiled at her. "That's

right, honey. That's why I decided we are going to move out there."

"Move out to Walnut Park? Harry Davis, have you gone clean out of your senses?" She was really excited.

My father got up and came around the table to her. He rested his hands on her shoulders. "Now, Martha, calm down and listen, will you? I've been doing some serious thinking about our future. You've been saying yourself that the city's no longer a good place to raise kids. Well, I agree with that. We both want the best for our kids, don't we? We don't want them getting mugged on the way home from school. I want Freddie and Candy to have opportunities—the sort of chances we never had, Martha! I want them to get a good education, see open space and green hills, and breathe fresh, clean air."

My dad was getting pretty worked up by now, and I wondered if we were in for one of my parents' rare shouting matches. But then Mom started gazing up at Dad with a dreamy look in her eyes. "Well, Harry, it would be kind of nice to have a real backyard," she said. "I could grow my own vegetables and flowers. I've always dreamed of a real garden."

"We could plant a peach tree, just like your mama has," Dad added, and there they were, both in the middle of a happy daydream about all the outdoor things they were going to do. They were going to ride bikes and take picnics and be real country folks.

Freddie and I just sat there and stared at them. They seemed to have forgotten all about us. Then Freddie spoke up.

"You two can do what you want," he said. "But I'm not coming with you."

Mom and Dad came down off their little cloud and looked surprised.

"You can't expect me to move in the middle of my senior year," Freddie said. "I've got college to think about. I won't get that basketball scholarship if I move to a new school. Besides, I'd never make friends."

"He's right, Harry," Mom said after a minute's silence. "It wouldn't be fair to move him now. We'll have to arrange for him to stay with friends during the week, and he can come home to us on weekends."

"That sounds like a great idea," I said. "I'll do that, too. I can stay with Bobby V."

Dad smiled but shook his head very firmly. "No way, young lady," he said. "I'm not letting you out of my sight for five days at a time. Especially not with that Roberta girl. She's a wild one—too wild for you."

"Oh, Dad, she's not. She's just fun, that's

4

all," I said fiercely. "Besides, I don't want to go to a new school, either. It was bad enough getting used to one high school. Now I finally know my way around, and you want me to start all over again. That's not fair."

"Well, Candy, you're just a freshman. The sooner you move and make new friends the better," Dad said. "And who was it who was always going on about how filthy Lincoln High is? Just do some sensible thinking. Think of a new school with lots of windows and green fields, fine teachers, good sports—"

"I'm useless at sports, remember?" I interrupted. "Freddie's the athlete, not me."

"You should be good at basketball now that you've shot up, stringbean," Freddie said. "I can't think why you didn't want to try out for the team. If you keep growing at this rate, you'll be able to *drop* the ball into the basket."

"Very funny," I snapped. "You know I can't run fast. You have to run to play basketball. I always trip over my feet or do something embarrassing."

"But, Candy, there will be all sorts of new sports out there in Walnut Park," Dad said. "They have a swimming pool and softball and goodness knows what else. You're bound to find something you like."

"Nothing will be any fun if I don't know

anybody," I said miserably. "And no one will ever want to make friends with me."

Dad smiled as if he understood. "Look, honey," he said softly, "the longer you're in high school, the harder it will be to transfer. You're just going to have to be brave and face up to it now. All right, who says we go house hunting on Saturday?"

Only my mother answered.

Chapter Two

The first thing that struck me about Walnut Park was not the view of the green Southern California hills or the new shopping malls or the nice, clean suburban houses with big lawns. It was the fact that all the other people were white.

"They won't even want us here," I muttered to Freddie. His curiosity had gotten the better of him, so he'd come along for the ride.

My father, who has unnaturally good hearing, particularly when you don't want him to hear, turned around and said, "The plant manager says that all kinds of folks are moving into Walnut Park. It's a new town, and everyone gets along just fine."

But I wasn't so sure. I didn't even get along "just fine" in my own neighborhood where I was born and raised. Out here, a five-foot-nine, skinny black girl would certainly stick out. I tried to point this out to Mom and Dad. I tried to point out every little disadvantage. "And how are you going to walk to the store, Mom? These shopping malls are not close to anything. And what will Grandma say when she finds out she's all alone in the city?"

But they had an answer for everything. It seemed that nothing would bring them down from their rosy cloud. They were like two little kids let loose in a toy store around Christmas time. I had never realized they wanted to have a vegetable garden, to ride bikes, and have barbeques. I guess I never realized that parents still had dreams. Anyway, my parents made it clear that now that they had found their dream, they were not going to let anything, even a brokenhearted, panic-stricken adolescent daughter, stand in their way.

The real estate salesman, with charm oozing out of even his oily hair, took us to house after house. My mother liked each one better than the last. I worked like crazy pointing out tiny closets and dust-collecting corners, trees that were going to fall on the roof in the next storm, and basements that were sure to flood. But none of these things worried my mother. I kept praying that the prices would be much too high, that we'd never be able to find a house we could afford, that the neighbors would make it clear they didn't want a black family moving in. But nothing worked. When they found the house they liked, I watched them signing papers—actually signing my life away.

As we walked out of the house, a girl came out of the house next door. She had long ginger hair and a lot of freckles. She took a look at me and smiled.

"Hi!" she said as she ran down the street.

She looked like she was about my age. I wondered if we would become friends.

"So that's how it is," I told Bobby V. that night. "The trouble is, I can't even say that I hate it. The people are really friendly, and the house is a whole lot better than this one. I even get a bathroom all to myself while Freddie's away. And you can see hills from my bedroom window. My folks can't understand why I don't want to move. They think I'm crazy."

"Well, I think you're crazy, too," Bobby V. said, stretching out on my bed like a cat. "I'd move out of this dump like a shot if I could."

"Well, it's different for you," I said. "You get

along with people. You make friends easily. You're not scared of anything."

She grinned, showing all those big, white, even teeth. "That's right, you better believe it," she said. "Fearless, that's me."

That was true enough. Bobby V.—or, as she was originally named, Roberta Victoria Pearson—had had a very different sort of life from me, and as a result she acted pretty different. When she was only seven, her father had deserted her family. She had two little brothers, so she'd had to take on the duties of mother while her own mother held down two jobs.

So she was able to handle a lot of things. She was tough and unafraid of anybody or anything. I'd grown up scared of most things. My world was a little, secure one of four quiet city blocks—all nice, brightly painted wooden houses with tiny backyards. My elementary school was just around the corner. When I came back from school, my mother was home to greet me. Grandma—my favorite person in the whole world—was only two streets away, in a tiny white house with a peach tree in her backyard.

So until high school, my life was a nice, quiet routine of school, home-baked food, and visits to Grandma. I thought it would go on forever.

But suddenly everything changed. I finished eighth grade and had to face high school. Abe Lincoln High was way across town in a strange, new world. About the time I was due to start high school, my grandmother fell and broke her hip, and my Aunt Marleen had to move in to look after her. Aunt Marleen was a grouchy old woman and didn't make me feel welcome at Grandma's. She kept telling me not to sit on the pillows, not to drop crumbs, and wasn't it about time that I went home?

Then, worst of all, I started to grow. Not just grow like any other teenager, but up, and up, and up. Not out, and out, either. I was still as skinny as any little kid, with less figure than a boy, but I was now five foot nine, and horribly conscious of it.

"Don't stoop," my mother kept nagging. "Stand up straight and be proud of yourself."

That was easy for her to say—at five foot five and nicely plump, you can bet nobody giggled when she walked past.

That was how I met Bobby V. in the first place, about two days into high school. Lincoln was a tough school, full of streetwise kids who pushed you out of their way and trampled you if you happened to be walking in the wrong direction down the hall. I was terrified. The school was a big, ugly brick building three floors high, and every hall looked like every other one. I thought of tying a string to my locker and unwinding it as I walked so that I could find my way back.

On the third morning I was desperately trying to remember where math was supposed to be—surely two-eighteen was on the second floor? I guess I was just standing in the middle of the hall, looking dumb and lost, when a group of tough kids came along.

"Hey, who put a telephone pole here?" one of the boys yelled. He was built like a football player, with great big shoulders and a huge Afro on a giant head. He looked terrifying.

"That's not a telephone pole, dummy," another boy, taller and skinnier but still pretty tough-looking, answered. "See, it's got hair on top!" And he flicked at my short curls.

"Oh—that's hair—my mistake," the first boy said, peering closely at me. "I thought it was a bird's nest."

They all burst out laughing as if they thought they were very witty. I didn't know what to do. I was about to cry, and I fought to stop myself. In a panic, I looked around like a trapped animal trying to find a way out. But they were all around—big, tough kids—powerful and sure of themselves—all laughing at me.

Just then a voice came echoing down the hall—a loud, strong girl's voice. "All right, Wilt Thompson, what do you think you're doing?"

Then a girl pushed her way through the crowd until she was standing next to me. She was a dainty, frail-looking girl with enormous dark eyes, an elaborate hairdo, and a brilliant red shirt. Her black eyes flashed dangerously as she looked from one kid to the next.

"You need a hearing aid, Wilt Thompson?" she said. "I asked you a question, and you didn't answer me. I asked you what you were doing?" The big boy lowered his eyes and looked uncomfortable.

"Nothing much," he mumbled.

"It had better *be* nothing much," the girl retorted. "And you'd better stay clear of this girl in the future because she's my friend. You hear me?"

"Sure, Bobby V.," he mumbled. "Come on, you guys." And they all drifted away.

Now Bobby V. turned those flashing eyes on me. "What do you have to say for yourself, then?" she demanded. "You don't just stand there and let them walk all over you. You got to stand up for yourself at this school, or they'll eat you alive. Do I make myself clear?"

I nodded.

She looked hard at me. I think she saw the tear that had started to trickle down my cheek. "What's your name, girl?" she asked.

"Candy Davis," I mumbled.

"Well, Candy Davis, it seems to me as though you need someone to show you around," she said. "Come on." She jerked her head, and I followed. From that day on she was my protector, guide, and friend.

Having Bobby V. for a friend was a wonderful new world. I'd never really had a best friend before. I'd gotten along OK with the kids in school. I got asked to the average number of parties, and nobody actually hated me, but I'd never had someone to share things with—a real, true best friend.

It was funny how opposite we were—I was tall, skinny, clumsy, and shy—and Bobby V. was short, outgoing, and friendly. But we seemed to provide each other with the side of ourselves that was lacking. She loved coming around to our house and soaking up the peace and orderliness after the chaos of her own house. My parents made it quite clear that they didn't like her from the first. "That loud-mouthed kid," my father called her; and my mother, who could never find anything really bad to say about people, simply called her, "Not Candy's type at all."

All that was true. She was a loudmouth. She'd yell things at boys across a street, and she was always getting in trouble in school for sassing teachers and talking in class. But she was fun and had a very kind heart. She was like a ray of dazzling light. And now she wouldn't be there anymore.

"What am I ever going to do without you?" I said, wailing.

Bobby V. smiled. "You make it sound like you're going to Alaska instead of fifty miles away. We can visit some weekends, and I'll write. I've always wanted a pen pal. Now I can have one. I'll write during world history class— you know how bored I get. It will stop me from getting into trouble for talking."

"But how will I ever make friends? All those white kids won't want to know me. And as for getting a boyfriend—I'll probably die an old maid!"

Bobby V. laughed. "Nothing to it, girl. You just smile and act friendly, and everyone will be friendly to you. That works for boys and girls, for black people and white people. At least, it's always worked for me," she said proudly. "And I can get any boy I want!" she added with a foxy-lady wiggle.

"Yes, but you're *you*," I said, sighing. "I always clam up and can't think of anything to say."

Bobby V.'s eyes lit up. "Boy, I wish I was going to that school," she said. "Anything would be better than the dump we go to!"

"I wish you were coming," I said. "Maybe I can persuade my parents to adopt you."

She laughed. "And who would look after little Matt and Dougie, I'd like to know. Although, I must say, I'd almost sell my soul for a bathroom of my own!"

Chapter Three

Suddenly my life seemed to be a speeded-up, fast action film. Only the thought of that bathroom—pale pink tiled and all to myself (except on weekends)—kept me going. Our old house was full of boxes, and my mother had packed away everything I wanted. Utter confusion.

Then the big moving truck came, and bit by bit we emptied our house of all our belongings, leaving memories glaring from the exposed walls—the notch where I ran into a doorway once on my new tricycle, the almost invisible crayon marks where I first printed my name on the kitchen wall—and got a spanking for it—and the shadow on the bedroom ceiling that sometimes turned into a monster in the middle of the night. Now that

17

monster looked down at me almost sadly, as if it would miss me, too.

"Come on, Candy! Where is that child! Candy—we're waiting to leave!" my mother called. I turned and tried not to look back as I walked out.

On the way to Walnut Park I tried to psych myself up by thinking of all the good things about my new life—the view from my bedroom window (I had to admit that the hills would be pretty, especially when the sun rose over them), that clean, pink bathroom, the shiny new high school with no graffiti on the walls and no broken windows, the community swimming pool only a block away—but after each item came the nagging *And no friends!*

For two days after we arrived, I was too busy unpacking boxes and moving furniture to think about myself at all. I was so tired at night that I flopped into bed and didn't move until morning. Then the third day came, the house was more or less in order, Dad went off to work at his new job, and it all came back to me: the next day I would start at that new high school. My stomach felt as if I had just stepped into an elevator shaft.

In the middle of the morning, my mother sent me to the store for some things she'd forgotten. She still hadn't gotten used to the big once-a-week shopping at the supermarket after having had a corner store to run to all her life. Although the supermarket was sort of far away, I didn't make a fuss about going. First, I knew that Mom was tired enough without trekking to the store. She had worked harder than anyone packing and unpacking, and she needed a rest. And second, it would give me a chance to check out the neighborhood and see if it was true that we were the only black family in Walnut Park. It sure seemed that way.

As I came out of the front door, I saw the girl from the next house working in her front yard. She was down on her knees pulling weeds, and it made me think that people don't talk about the extra chores that come with big yards. Next week it would probably be *me* pulling weeds, I said to myself. The girl looked up as she heard our door close and gave me a big smile.

"Oh, hi, it's you," she said. "I saw the moving truck and wanted to come over, but Mom said you'd be too busy to want visitors for a few days."

"We're all straightened out now," I said. "Come over if you want to."

"Good, I will," she said. "Boy, you don't

know how glad I am that you moved in here. There are no other kids my age on this whole block, and the old neighbors used to complain if I played my stereo after eight P.M. By the way, I'm Ginger Marshall."

"I'm Candy Davis."

"What grade are you in, Candy?" she asked.

"I'm a freshman."

"Me, too. I wonder if we'll have any of the same classes?"

"I don't know what my classes are yet," I said. "I have to see the principal tomorrow."

"Well, don't let him put you in Hammond's English class." She giggled. "They spent a whole semester building an igloo with sugar cubes and writing poems in the shape of flowers."

I smiled. "Sounds easier than grammar."

"Yeah, but not much use when you get a hard teacher in soph English," Ginger replied. "You want to come in and have a soda? I'd use any excuse to stop digging up dandelions," she said, standing up stiffly. "Oh, my aching back. Child abuse. Coke or Seven Up?"

"Thanks, but I'd better not stop right now," I said, hoping she wouldn't think I was snubbing her. "You see, I told my mother I'd run down to the store for her. She keeps finding groceries we're out of, and she wants to get started on dinner."

"That's what happens when you move," Ginger said. "I remember when we moved here it took ages to get straightened out. Did you move from out of state?"

"All the way from the city," I said. "At least forty miles away, but it feels like a different planet."

Ginger smiled as if she understood, and I felt a leap of hope that perhaps it wasn't going to be so lonely out here. "Yeah," she said, "I guess life is really different in the city. I've never tried it. I've been in one suburb after another—same type of house, same supermarkets all across the country. My dad gets transferred about every three years, then we pack up and move to an identical house a thousand miles away, and I have to fit in all over again. It doesn't make sense, does it?"

I shook my head. "That's how I feel exactly," I said. "I'm dreading starting at a new school here."

"You don't have to," Ginger said. "It really isn't as bad as all that. Not as schools go."

There was a pause. I took a deep breath and got up the nerve to ask the question I was dying to ask.

"Er—Ginger—I've been wondering if there

21

are—er—many black kids—at your school? I mean, do they all—does everyone—get along OK?"

She smiled understandingly, and I felt a whole lot better even before she answered. "You don't have to worry," she said. "Everyone gets along real well out here. It's a new town, and I suppose nobody can say they got here first, so there aren't any bad feelings at school. There aren't a whole lot of black kids, though, and they tend to stick together quite a bit. There are these two girls named Helen Franklin and Diana Oates. They're like the leaders. If they think you're OK, you're in."

Just then a yell came from inside the house. Ginger looked up. "I'd better go," she said. "That's my dad yelling. I bet he just needs another beer, and he won't leave the ball game on TV! Talk about the family workhorse! Oh, well, see you at school tomorrow, Candy. Bye." Then she ran into the house. I continued down the street slowly. For a while there, I'd felt pretty hopeful about the new school and everyone being friendly. I just wished Ginger hadn't told me about Helen and Diana and how they had to like you—because the chances were that they wouldn't like me one bit, and I'd never be in with anyone at all.

I walked past rows of identical front lawns,

all nicely mowed, with bikes carelessly left in driveways. Kids were washing cars in many of the driveways. It looked like a friendly, relaxed sort of place, I had to admit, and Ginger couldn't have been nicer—but I still couldn't help feeling nervous. Most of all, I missed Bobby V. What fun would it be going to school if Bobby V. wasn't there? Even if I did make friends, I knew I'd never have a best friend again—the sort of friend that you know so well you don't have to think before you speak, who understands when you're feeling down and knows just the right thing to say to make you feel better. I decided I'd write a letter to Bobby V. as soon as I got back from the store.

My father offered to drive me to school on the first day, but I chose to walk. Walking was more invisible, and I wanted to be as invisible as possible that day. I'd already planned things out. I'd slink up to the main gate, and if I didn't see any other black kids, I'd slink home again and sign up for a high-school correspondence course, which I'd take hidden in my new private bathroom.

As it happened, almost the first kids I saw, standing together on the school lawn, were black. I saw them as I walked past the elegant wrought-iron fence, so different from the high wire-and-concrete one that wrapped around Lincoln High. These black kids were standing together in a cozy little group, about a dozen boys and girls. As I walked through the gate, I noticed that a couple of the boys had their arms draped over girls' shoulders. They had their heads close together as if they were sharing a story or joke. I guess it must have been a joke because they broke apart, laughing loudly. Then one of the girls turned away, saying, "You are terrible, Peter Willis. I don't believe a word of it, and you're making me late for geometry."

One look at her told me that this must be Helen or Diana. She looked like something straight out of a Coke commercial—tall, slim, but not too slim, with skin a fantastic light coffee color, and big dark eyes. She walked toward me like a model in a fashion show, her hips swaying, showing off her Calvin Kleins that looked as though she'd been poured into them.

She seemed to know that she was great-looking and that everybody was watching her. And she was enjoying it.

When she was a few paces away from me, she stopped and looked back. "You coming, Helen?" she called. OK, so this was Diana.

Another girl moved away from the group, almost as stunning as Diana, though much shorter and more bouncy. Her hair was braided with millions of glass beads that flashed as she turned her head. When she called out, "All right, don't rush me," in her smooth, deep voice, she flashed a bright, white smile.

They passed right by me, and I guess I just stood there like a dummy and gaped at them. I suppose I hoped for a miracle, that one of them would notice me and say, "Oh, you're new here, aren't you? Let us show you around." When it was clear that they were not going to notice me, something inside me whispered that I should stop them and introduce myself. I should go right up to them and say, "Hi, I'm Candy and I'm new here and somebody said I should get in touch with you two."

But even as I was thinking these thoughts and knowing in my heart that I would never have the nerve to say them aloud, Diana and Helen swept past me as though I didn't exist. With their two queens gone, the rest of the group drifted off in different directions, and I was left alone on the empty path. The sinking feeling of panic was stronger than ever now.

All right, I thought, I'm going home and taking high school by mail.

But then a bell rang, reminding me that I had a nine o'clock appointment with the principal and that he might phone my mother if I didn't show up. I decided that an angry mother might not be the best thing to face right then, so I turned and plodded up the front steps.

So I'll spend the rest of my life eating sandwiches alone in a corner, I thought. So I'll never belong to a group, never be part of the "in crowd," never have a boyfriend—so what? Who cares? Then the little voice came back, *I care. I care a whole lot.* But I knew full well that I had as much chance of being part of Helen and Diana's group as I did of being chosen Miss Black America of 1983!

The principal was nice enough. He was a fussy little man who didn't look a bit like a principal and who said "er" and "ah" between words. He gave me a long speech about being welcome and how the kids were friendly and how I'd soon feel like I belonged, and then he shipped me across to a counselor, who managed to fit all the required classes into my schedule whether I wanted them or not.

The kids seemed nice enough too. Some of them even offered to share their books with me when I joined their classes. Ginger passed me in the halls with a group of friends and called out, "Hi," but she didn't stop to introduce me to her friends.

Well, of course I can't expect to get to know people the first day, I told myself. But I didn't look forward to lunch hour when everyone else sat with their friends and I sat alone in the corner like Cinderella.

The period before lunch I had biology. I had never taken biology before. At Lincoln High I was in general science, but here there was only biology, physics, or chemistry. I thought biology sounded a bit less scary than the other two. When I walked into the laboratory, everyone was already busy at benches, and the place stank of something disgusting. I stood in the doorway not knowing what to do. Quite frankly, I wanted to turn right around and go out again rather than stay with that smell.

But before I could do anything of the kind, the teacher spotted me. "Hey, you," he boomed. "You're late. Don't just stand there. Sit down and get started."

I tried to say, "I don't know where to sit," but that man made me feel so nervous, the words wouldn't come out.

He glared at me and roared, "Are you deaf or something? I said go to your place and get to work." I felt like I was in a nightmare, that my knees wouldn't hold me up any longer.

"But I don't have a place yet," I mumbled. "I'm new."

"What are you mumbling on about?" he snapped. "I can't hear a word you're saying. Are you trying to tell me you've forgotten your assignment or something?"

"No, Mr. Dalton, she's new, and she doesn't know our program," a voice from the back yelled. The other kids all giggled. Mr. Dalton looked from the kid in the back to me and back again.

"You're new to this class?" he asked.

I nodded.

"Well, why didn't you say so?" he said. "What's your name?"

"Candy Davis," I murmured.

"You have to speak up in this class," he said. "I don't like mumbling. I won't tolerate it. Very well, find a seat and get someone to show you what we're doing, Candy."

"Come on back here," the kid at the back called. "You can share with me."

"That's enough noise from you, Helen," Mr. Dalton said. "I can always hear you *too* clearly!"

I didn't care what Mr. Dalton said or did anymore. All I knew was that Helen was in the back row and she wanted me to sit beside her. I almost hugged Mr. Dalton for being so mean and stupid. I hurried past the rows of benches and gratefully sank down beside Helen.

"Thanks for rescuing me," I whispered.

"Don't mind him," she said.

"Is he always so mean?" I asked.

"He should have retired years ago." She grinned. "He's half-blind, half-deaf, and can't remember a thing anymore. He yelled at you because he thought you were me, and I do come in a little late from time to time."

"How could he mistake me for you?" I asked. Helen, as I've said before, was around five foot two and bouncy.

Helen grinned again.

We both giggled.

"What did you say your name was?" she whispered.

"Candy."

"I'm Helen," she said. "And we better get started on dissecting this frog, or Dalton's going to start yelling again."

"You mean cut it up?" I asked, looking in horror at the flabby dead frog and the scalpels on the table.

"It's not as bad as it sounds," she said. "Just watch me."

I did watch her. She was very clever with

that knife, and she worked fast. Soon we had bits of neatly labeled frog spilling over the table. Even Mr. Dalton had to admit we were doing a good job.

But the best thing of all happened at the end of the period. As we were washing that revolting dead frog smell from our hands, Helen said, "Do you have someone to eat lunch with yet? If not, why don't you come over and meet the rest of the kids?"

Chapter Four

Going to meet the rest of Helen's group that lunchtime reminded me of my eighth-grade graduation. I had felt happy and excited and, at the same time, scared to death I would do something dumb like trip over my feet. That's exactly how I felt when the kids looked up as Helen brought me toward them.

"Guess who I found in biology today!" she called happily.

"She looks sort of alive to me," one of the boys quipped. "I thought everything you found in biology was dead. Do we get to dissect her?"

"Don't be disgusting, George," Helen said. She turned to me. "He thinks he's real witty— a real funny guy. But don't you take him seriously. He's just a tease." She linked her arm through his, saying emphatically to me, "This one is mine, Candy."

"Well, aren't you going to introduce the rest of us?" Diana said sharply. Her big black eyes looked at me as if she didn't want me there at all. She seemed mad at Helen for bringing me.

"Everybody," Helen said, "this is Candy Davis. She just moved here from the city, and she's a freshman. Candy, this is Diana and Walt, Sharron and Mike, Crissy and Peter, Ann and Bob, and Jennifer and Matt."

All those twosomes, I thought bleakly. It sounds like she's counting off Noah's Ark. I can't fit in here. I'll always be odd girl out.

That was obviously what Diana thought because she said, "Are you going with someone yet, Candy?"

"I've only been here four days," I said, laughing and meeting her cool gaze. "Give me a chance."

"We'll have to see if we can find someone for you," she said and gave me a smile that didn't manage to reach her eyes. "Helen, what nice, unattached young men do we know in this dump?"

"I don't need you to do that," I interrupted, feeling a little braver now that she was treating me like something to be pitied. "I'm sure

I can find my own boy when I've been here long enough to meet kids."

"Yeah, Diana," Helen said. "Just cool it. It's only her first day here. You can hardly expect her to walk up to the first cute boy she sees and say 'I'm new here, will you go out with me?' And besides, when she gets to know kids, she will find that there are no *nice* boys in this school!"

"Present company excepted," George said quickly.

"Present company definitely not excepted," Helen returned.

"Well, you seem to find me nice enough." He grinned.

"That's only because there's nothing better around," Helen said smugly, but she gave his arm a little squeeze to show that she was just teasing.

I felt a stupid stab of jealousy watching them. Would I ever have a boyfriend like that—a guy I could feel comfortable with and could tease without his taking it the wrong way? One thing at a time, I reproached myself. First worry about making some friends. You can worry about boys later.

But Diana still stared at me coldly as she slowly, smoothly slipped her arm around Walt's waist. Her eyes seemed to tell me to take the next flight to the moon. Then the thought came to me in a flash. She's jealous. She's afraid I'll steal her boyfriend.

The next thing I knew, the words had just popped right out of my mouth.

"Well, actually, I do sort of have a boyfriend back in the city." As soon as I'd said it, I wished I hadn't. To hide my feelings, I opened my purse and rummaged for my comb. As I brought it out, an envelope fluttered to the floor. George bent down to pick it up and glanced at it as he handed it to me. It was a letter from Bobby V., with her name and return address printed clearly in her bold handwriting.

"Hey, gang, look what I found. Bobby V., huh? I bet it's a letter from her boyfriend." He kept holding it out to me, but somehow my hands wouldn't take it. Finally he threw it on the lunch table. I was so scared I couldn't even move.

Then Diana unwrapped her arm from around Walt and picked up the letter. She slipped it out of the envelope and began to read out loud:

Dear Candy,
I miss you already. There won't be anyone else to share secrets the way

we did. What am I going to do with myself on weekends? I know your folks don't like me too much and that they think I'm a wild, terrible influence on you, whatever that means, so I bet I won't ever get invited to visit you. But I hope you'll come back and visit me. Remember the fun times we had late at night when my family was all asleep?

Yours always,
Bobby V.

George burst out laughing. "Hey, this sounds like *some* guy!"

I felt just awful. I opened my mouth to say, "It's not a guy at all, it's a girl. Just my best friend at my old school. You've got it all wrong." But instead I heard myself saying, "Well, I guess he is pretty wild. But he's a lot of fun."

Chapter Five

When I was a little girl, my grandma used to tell me stories about kids who told lies and the terrible things that happened to them. "People who tell lies always come to a bad end," she would say every time I stretched the truth a little or fibbed that I *didn't* take the last cookie. I guess my grandma had done a good job of drumming that into my head, because I felt really bad that evening.

How can you have been so dumb? I asked myself over and over. Why didn't you come right out and tell the truth? No good can come of this. One day you'll get found out and look like a fool, and until then you won't ever be able to get it off your conscience.

Of course, I wasn't really the one who had lied, I argued to myself. They were the ones who said the letter came from my boyfriend. I just didn't tell them they were wrong. And besides, I argued further, the liar in Grandma's stories always said things that got other people into trouble. This lie didn't hurt anyone. In fact it helped everybody. The girls in the group were a lot more friendly when they knew I wasn't after their boyfriends, and Diana looked at me with new respect when she knew that I went with a "wild guy." I'd seen her coldness melt away as she read the letter. In fact, if she hadn't seen that letter from Bobby V., it was quite probable that she wouldn't have wanted me to join them again, and I would have blown my one chance for making friends. Everything was just great, and there was no way that anybody could get hurt—so why did I feel so bad?

True, the bad feeling didn't last long. I had one night of lying awake, feeling hot and embarrassed, staring at a ceiling that was white and smooth with no monsters on it, and wondering what would happen if I got found out. But after that I was too busy enjoying my new popularity to have time to feel guilty or worried.

Diana particularly was interested in finding out about Bobby V. She told me she had always wanted to go with a wild guy. She said all the boys in Walnut Park were safe and dependable and *boring*. She guessed life must be much more exciting in the city. (If she only knew how exciting my life in the city had been—all those wild checkers games and thrilling evenings watching TV.)

My English teacher back in Lincoln had always said that I used imagination and not enough grammar. Now my imagination came in very handy. I used it to create an imaginary Bobby V., leading an imaginary wild city life. If they could have seen me in the city, I often thought, scared to walk home in the dark from my grandma's house, scared to talk to anyone at school. But they didn't know. They thought I'd zoomed through city streets on a motorcycle behind a boy wearing a black leather jacket.

The kids at Walnut High were very impressed, and even I was kind of impressed by myself. My parents were amazed at the new me, especially when George and Helen called for me in the morning in George's car.

"I never believed you'd make friends that fast," my mother said. "To tell the truth, I was a bit worried about you fitting in here."

"You see?" my father said, beaming in triumph. "Didn't I tell you it was a friendly neighborhood?"

At the end of the week, I began to see that my new popularity was not going to be all smooth going. Helen had volleyball practice after school every day, and on Friday she asked me along.

"You should come, Candy," she coaxed. "With your height you'd be great to have on the team."

"Oh, I've never even played volleyball," I protested.

"It's easy," Helen said, "and it's fun, too. You'll soon pick it up."

"She's not telling the whole truth," Diana said, teasing. "What she doesn't tell you is the main reason she goes out for volleyball is the coach."

"Well, you must admit he is totally awesome," Helen said, sighing.

"Yeah, I guess he *is* radical," Diana agreed.

Those were two new words to me. I didn't know if they were meant to mean something good or bad. But from the dreamy look in Helen's eyes, I guessed they were meant to be good.

"Who is this coach?" I asked. "One of the teachers?"

"No way," Helen said. "You wouldn't find us wasting time over a teacher. This guy's a senior, and he's totally—"

"I know," I said, laughing, "he's totally radical and awesome, but however radical and awesome he is still doesn't change the fact that I can't play volleyball."

"It really isn't hard," Helen said. "And Jonathan really could use some new talent on the team. What do you say?"

"Well, I don't know," I said hesitantly. If these girls had ever watched me playing basketball, they'd know I didn't exactly move with the speed of light. I was pretty sure I wouldn't be a whiz kid at volleyball, either. Also, it went without saying that any awesome and radical coach was not going to notice quiet little stringbean me.

"Oh, come on, Candy," Diana said. "We all go along to practice. Some of us who aren't such superjocks—like me, for one—sit and watch, and then afterward we all go to the deli for ice cream. It's like the big Friday night Walnut Park social activity. After all, we're not in the big city, and this rates for excitement out here. You going to come with us?"

Of course I would have been a fool to say no when she put it like that. After all, this was what I had been dreaming of all my life—to belong to a group of kids, to be wanted, to be liked. And this wasn't any old group of kids.

This was the group that mattered if you were black at Walnut High. The fact that I couldn't play volleyball didn't seem to be important. What I cared about was fitting in with Helen and Diana's plans.

It wasn't until we were walking across to the gym after school that I thought about volleyball again. Everyone else was talking loudly and laughing and making jokes. I began to feel scared. What if they made me play volleyball? What would the coach say when he saw me play? Obviously he'd say, "Get out of here, you have no idea how to play this game!"

So I won't play, I argued with myself. I'll just sit and watch with Diana. If she doesn't play, I don't have to.

It was cool and dark in the gymnasium, and the building echoed with the thud of a heavy ball and an occasional female scream.

"Come on, Helen, you're late as usual," said the coach as he approached us.

"Sorry, Jonathan," Helen said, purring. "But I know you'll forgive me when I tell you the good news—I've found you a fantastic new player!"

"Oh, that's terrific," he said, smiling down at me. "Hi, there," he said. "I'm Jonathan Robbins." I didn't say anything. My vocal cords would not work for the simple reason that Jonathan Robbins was about the cutest guy I had ever seen. He was tall—at least six-three. You could see he was an athlete. Muscles positively rippled under his T-shirt. His hair was in a short Afro, and warm, black eyes sparkled over high cheekbones in an ebony-dark face.

"This is Candy Davis," I heard Helen saying for me.

Jonathan stuck out a huge brown hand. "Glad to meet you, Candy," he said in a deep, rumbling voice.

It was all I could do to make my own hand move. When it touched his, I felt as if someone had turned on a thousand-volt current.

"Where have you played before, Candy?" he asked. "I could sure use a spiker with your height."

"Look, I have to tell you something," I managed to stammer. "I've never even played before. I kept telling Helen that, but she wanted me to come along anyway."

"Helen knows I always want to check out new *talent*," he said, emphasizing the last word.

"You can cut that out, Jonathan," Helen said severely. "She's already got a guy of her own, and he's tough and rides motorcycles and wears leather jackets."

"OK, I get your drift," Jonathan said quickly. "Don't worry—my interest is purely professional, I promise." He gave me a long, interested look, then added, "And I don't mess with guys in leather jackets."

I began to see that there were other punishments for telling lies. One of them was having the cutest guy in the world think I was not available. I wanted to speak up right then, to tell him I'd made the whole thing up or that my tough boyfriend had miraculously been killed in a motorcycle crash only hours before, but before I had time to collect my thoughts, Jonathan became the coach again—strict and businesslike.

"All right, Candy Davis—get on the court. Let's see what you can do," he barked. "And you others, I want to see some action, not a bunch of wooden dummies standing there. I want to see dives at the ball. Remember, you're players, not a forest of trees!"

Feeling like a complete fool, I followed Helen to the back of the court. I hoped that if I was far enough back, the ball would never get to me. Then the game started. Someone on my right sent the ball zinging over the net, and someone punched it back, then it went over again. They all acted very quick and strong. Thirteen female jocks and me. Even Helen, although she was short, was clearly a good player. She moved quickly and flung herself at the ball as if she didn't think about getting hurt.

Then someone else served, and we all changed places, and I found myself getting nearer and nearer the net. At last I was standing right in the middle of the court, feeling like one of those ducks that goes up and down at a rifle range at a fair. The server sent the ball flying, someone knocked the ball back, and then it came zooming straight toward my face. Of course I put my hand up to stop it from hitting me, and when I looked again, everyone was saying, "Great shot, Candy!"

After that I began to feel a bit more hopeful, and several times I found that I could reach a ball the other girls couldn't. Then it was my turn to serve. I had watched how the other girls did it. It looked simple. You just punched it over with your fist. I tried it. Until then I didn't realize how hard the ball was or how soft human fists were. The ball didn't even make it over the net, and my wrist felt as if I had just punched a brick wall.

"Try it again, Candy," Jonathan called. "Hit

it harder this time. Real hard. Put some muscle into it."

I tried hard. I put all my strength into that next serve. I don't quite know what went wrong. Maybe I let go of the ball at the wrong moment, for it zoomed off to the right and hit Jonathan right on the head. The other girls all burst out laughing.

"I'm sorry," I stammered, feeling so embarrassed I wanted to die. "But I *did* try to tell you I wouldn't be any good at this." I turned away from the net and walked toward the bleachers. "You'd better put someone else in, and I'll just sit here and watch," I said.

"Candy Davis, you get back here," Jonathan roared. "You're quick, and you're strong, and you have the height I need. If I survive long enough without getting a concussion, I'm going to make you into a great volleyball player!"

Chapter Six

I don't know why I ever thought Jonathan was cute, because he turned out to be a monster disguised as a volleyball coach. I don't know why I didn't quit volleyball, either, because I hated it. Every afternoon I dreaded going to that gym and getting bruises all over me while Jonathan yelled. It was not my idea of a fun afternoon at all, but every time I tried to talk to him about quitting, he just wouldn't listen. He was such a bully that I found myself returning again and again, rather than have Jonathan mad at me.

"Look at me," I said to my mother as I emerged from the shower. "My hands are bruised from hitting that stupid ball, my side and my rear end are bruised from those dives and rolls he makes us do, I have about four fingers practically dislocated, and all my toes are stubbed. If ever I wanted to claim child abuse, this would be the perfect time to do it."

My mother smiled and went on folding the towels. "Nothing's easy till you get the hang of it," she said, calmly handing me a towel.

"I don't mind hard work," I said. "But that coach is a monster. He doesn't ever let us rest, and he yells at me more than the rest of them put together."

"He looked very nice to me that time I came by to pick you up," my mother said and went back to folding towels.

I grunted. "He may look nice," I said. "Even I have to admit he looks pretty cute, but under that cute exterior lurks one real mean guy."

My mother smiled. "In the end you'll thank him for it because you'll turn out to be a good player, and maybe you'll even get scholarships like your brother and be able to go to any college you want."

I rubbed my head with my towel and looked at her scornfully.

Funny enough, I got a letter from Bobby V. that day, a letter that made me smile bitterly.

This I must *see*. I can't imagine Candy Davis playing on a volleyball team! You never were too keen on any form of PE at school, but it sounds as if the coach has a lot to do with you taking up volleyball. He sounds really cute! One of these days I must come and see for myself—also to watch you flinging yourself around a court. What a laugh! Of course, you may be a superstar by the time I get to see you, unless you ever come to play a game in the city. Let me know if you ever do, hey?

I hope we can see each other before long. It seems like I have so much to tell you, but I'm writing this in world history as usual, and my mind is blank.

Regards (Love?!!!) to the coach. Some people get all the luck. If I went out for volleyball, the coach would be a fifty-five-year-old woman!

Love,
Bobby V.

I sighed and folded up the letter. Then I got a piece of paper and started to write back to her. "There have been certain developments since I wrote that last letter," I began. "That really cute coach has turned into Frankenstein. . . ."

As I went out to mail the letter, I saw Ginger. "I hear you're the rising star of the volleyball squad," she yelled to me from across the street so that the whole world could hear.

"Very funny," I said as she ran across to join me. "Anyone who has ever seen me play volleyball would not describe it that way. And anyway," I added, "who told you about the volleyball?"

"That's what happens when you go to a small school," Ginger said. "Everyone knows everything about everyone else. News gets around quicker than you would believe. If you dare stop and talk to a boy in the hall for one minute, rumor will have it that you're going together by lunchtime."

"I better watch who I talk to then," I said. "But who told you about me playing volleyball?"

"Oh, just this guy I know," she said vaguely. "He's in a class with Jonathan Robbins, and somehow your name came up."

I felt myself going hot and was immediately mad at myself. "Whoever said that was out of his skull," I growled. "All I have to show for three weeks of volleyball practice is bruises all over my body."

"About Jonathan Robbins," she said. "My friend said he sure talked about you a lot."

"Him!" I exploded. "He may be tall and handsome, but how can you feel romantic about someone who does nothing but yell at you!"

"Well, at least he notices you when he yells," Ginger said and sighed. "I joined the chess club because Brent Holmes—you know, that boy with the curly hair in our English class—plays chess. But he doesn't even notice I'm alive. The only time he talks to me is to say, 'Your move,' or 'checkmate.' " We both laughed.

"I have to go right now," Ginger said. "Have to fix dinner before my mom gets home from work. But you'll have to come over soon, and we'll play some records."

"Yeah, great," I said eagerly.

"Good. See ya," Ginger called and ran up the path to her house.

Well, that's one good thing that's happened to me already, I thought as I opened our front door. Until I moved here, I'd hardly ever spoken to a white girl. Now I was kidding around with Ginger as if I'd known her for years. And I felt like I was really beginning to belong to Helen and Diana's group. So, apart from Jonathan's yells and my bruised wrists, everything was going just fine. I had to admit, though grudgingly, that I was glad we had moved. Of course, I still missed Bobby V.

Thinking of Bobby V. reminded me that I still was keeping up my stupid lie. Every few days I had to invent a new letter or phone call from my "wild boyfriend," and to tell the truth, I was running out of ideas fast. I was even toying with a crazy scheme to kill him off in a fiery motorcycle crash, but that sort of thing would get around and somehow get back to my parents.

I hoped that Helen and the others liked me enough for myself to forget the pretend Bobby V. We talked about him less and less as the days passed. I never brought up the subject— and hoped they wouldn't.

That Friday we had a particularly tough workout. Mr. Mean Jonathan made us run across the court, punch the ball upward, and take a rolling dive. If it sounds pretty impossible, that's just how it was. Every time I rolled, the floor felt harder and harder.

"That hurts, Jonathan," I complained.

"Only because you're not falling properly," he said, showing no concern for my suffering at all. "Let your hip take the fall first. Show her, Melanie."

Melanie waddled over. She was a big, beefy girl who looked like she wore a size twenty-two and was fullback for the Rams in her spare time. She dove, bounced, and got back up.

"You see," Jonathan said. "It's easy. Now you try it."

I did, but it still hurt. "That's because Melanie is well padded, and I'm all skin and bones," I said.

"If you'd quit complaining and start working, you'd be some use to this team," Jonathan said. I glared at his back and sent out strong hate messages as he walked away.

An hour later I still ached all over. I could scarcely move my arm.

After practice we all went over to the World's Best, a neat deli that just happened to serve the world's best ice cream. Helen called it "awesome," of course. We were sitting around, sharing a Matterhorn sundae (eleven scoops and four toppings, plus whipped cream) when the subject of Bobby V. came up again.

"Would you pass me that napkin, please?" I asked Sharron. "My muscles simply won't work anymore."

"Tough workout, eh?" George asked, grinning.

"It's that Robbins. He's got it in for me," I said and groaned.

"That's not how I see it at all," Helen said,

grinning slyly. "It's clear to me that Jonathan likes you."

"Likes me?" I nearly choked on the butterscotch topping. "Whatever gave you that idea?"

"I just know he does, that's all," she said, digging into the butter pecan. "After all, you must admit he spends more time working with you than with anyone else."

"That's because I'm so much worse than anyone else," I said.

Helen shook her head. "It's not that. And you're not worse than us anymore. Jonathan checks out every little thing you do. If I hit the ball wrong, he doesn't say a thing, but with you he hits the ceiling."

"I wouldn't call that liking somebody," I said. "That's the way I would treat my worst enemy."

"But you must have noticed the way he looks at you," Helen insisted.

Suddenly I felt confused and embarrassed. I'd thought Helen was just kidding around, but now I saw that she meant it. She really did think Jonathan liked me. I thought it over for a minute. True, he had looked at me long and hard when we first met, but I put that down to sizing up a future player. He certainly yelled at me more than at the rest, but that sort of attention didn't mean somebody liked you. It just meant that you needed more coaching than the rest. And yet, as I thought some more, I began to wonder if she was right. There were times when his eyes did meet mine, just for a second. But no, I decided, she's crazy. If he really liked me, he'd have shown it more and yelled less.

"The only way I've seen him look at me is like a lion looks at a zebra before dinner," I said, and I dug into the ice cream.

Helen laughed. "I still think I'm right," she said. "I wonder what would happen if you met him somewhere where he wasn't the coach—maybe he'll come to the Spirit Week Dance?"

"Who, Jonathan?" Sharron butted in. "I didn't think he went in for social stuff like dancing."

"No, he's a strange one, Jonathan," Helen agreed after a moment. "Come to think of it, you never see him around much when he's not playing sports. He's not going with anyone, is he?"

"If he is, it's no one from school," Sharron said.

"Perhaps we should encourage him to get some other interests," Helen said. "Perhaps he wouldn't be so mean as a coach if volleyball wasn't the only thing in the world for him. Maybe that should be your job, Candy."

"What?" I asked, not really following.

"Well, since George here probably will not give me permission to make my coach's life more interesting—"

"You got it, baby," George put in quickly.

"As I was saying," Helen went on, "perhaps Candy should try to loosen up our friend Jonathan. Why don't you ask him to the dance?"

"Oh, but I couldn't—I don't even know if I want to—" I stammered. "I mean, when is this dance, what is it?"

"The Spirit Week Dance, why that's only two weeks away," Diana said, breaking off her conversation with the boys at the other end of the table and leaning across to join in ours. "But you mustn't put ideas into her head, Helen, about dancing with Jonathan. After all, she's already spoken for. Seems to me this is the right sort of occasion for us finally to meet the famous Bobby V."

I took a big bite of sundae. The nuts stuck in my throat, and I coughed.

"Hey, great idea," Helen said. "I was forgetting all about him. Of course you must bring him, Candy. I'm dying to see what he looks like."

"Yeah," Diana said, and a dreamy look came over her face. "I hope he comes on his motorcycle. He can take me for a little ride—"

"Look, you guys"—I faltered—"I don't know if he can come—I mean, it's a long way, and he doesn't get on with my parents—and—"

"Oh, I bet he'd come if you told him it was a special occasion and how your fabulous, great-looking new friends are all dying to meet him," Diana said.

"And especially if you tell him you'll have to invite Jonathan instead if he doesn't come," Helen added.

"If you're worried about your parents, why don't I phone them for you and ask them to be nice to him, just this once, as a favor to me," George added, butting in.

That did it. One thing I couldn't have was anyone phoning my parents. Somehow or other I had to produce a real live Bobby V. on the night of the dance or have a pretty good excuse why he couldn't be there.

Diana had finished her ice cream. She picked up her purse and slung it over her shoulder as she got up from the table. "Tell him he'd better be there," she said coolly, "or I'll start to believe he doesn't really exist."

Why couldn't I have said right there and then, "You're right. He doesn't exist." Instead

I scooped up another spoonful of ice cream, chocolate syrup, and chopped nuts and put it calmly into my mouth.

"Don't worry, Diana," I said, swallowing. "You've convinced me. I'll make sure I bring Bobby V. to the dance."

Chapter Seven

Some things are easier said than done. For example, I had just said I was bringing a nonexistent person to a dance. It was quite easy to say it, but not so easy to carry it out. I worried about it a lot. In fact, lying awake at night and staring at my monster-free ceiling, I tossed around a lot of ideas, some good and some not so good.

One of the best ideas was that I'd have a terrible fight with Bobby V. and break up with him two days before the dance. I'd be so upset that I'd hide in my room for days and not speak to anybody. The flaw in this idea was that the kids were bound to phone the house, and if I didn't manage to get to the phone first—no, that would never work!

Next idea—Bobby V. would have a motorcycle crash two days before the dance. Not a *fatal* crash, that would be too hard to deal with, but just enough of a crash to break his leg so he wouldn't come to the dance. That idea was a good one. If I didn't come up with anything better, it would have to do.

But at the back of my mind was a nagging doubt. Even if I explained away Bobby V. this time, I was going to have to produce him someday. Diana was beginning to sound suspicious. If they found out I was a great big fraud, who'd never even had a boyfriend, let alone a wild guy in a leather jacket, they'd drop me quick. And I didn't want that. I was having more fun now than I'd ever had. I liked these kids. True, Diana was a bit stuck-up and thought a lot of herself, but then so did all hotshots. And Helen was fun. So were George and the others. After a while I was even having a good time at volleyball. Not always, of course, and especially not on Jonathan's mean days. But I was learning what it was like to belong to a team, to feel that I mattered to other people and that they were glad to have me around. In volleyball people didn't laugh because I was tall. In fact, lots of players were almost as tall as me, and the shorter ones envied my height. "I can't reach that ball," they'd yell. "I'm not Candy, y'know!"

I didn't want to go back to being Miss Nobody again—the skinny stringbean who hid in corners and ate lunch alone. No, one thing was clear. Either I had to find some way of producing Bobby V. in two weeks' time or have a pretty good reason why I hadn't.

"You're an old worrywart these days," Ginger called over the fence. "Every time I see you, you're frowning. What's the tragedy?"

"Oh—nothing," I said, trying to make my face look calm and happy.

"Want to talk about it?" Ginger asked. "Maybe I could help."

I was very tempted at that moment to share my problem with her. It would have been so nice to say, "You see, I'm in this embarrassing situation, and I don't know what to do next," and spill the whole thing out to her. But something held me back. I just didn't know her well enough yet. Supposing she was a blabbermouth, and it was all over the school the next day? Supposing she thought I was terrible for lying like that and didn't want to be my friend anymore? Supposing she thought it was funny and teased me? There were too many supposings that sprang to my mind. No, however much I liked Ginger—and I did like her a lot—she was not yet a best friend like Bobby V. had been—the sort of best friend you could share any sort of problem with, no matter how embarrassing.

Suddenly I had an idea. Nobody was home. I could call Bobby V. right then and tell her. She'd know what to do. Bobby V. was always great at coming up with neat ideas. Even if the call was expensive, it was worth it.

"Thanks, Ginger, you've already helped," I said, and gave her a big smile. "Now I know what to do."

"What did I do?" I heard her calling as I ran into the house.

I can't tell you how wonderful it was to hear Bobby V.'s voice on the other end of that phone. "I thought you'd forgotten all about me now that you're living out in those fancy suburbs," she said.

"I do write," I said. "And it's not exactly cheap to phone."

"Only teasing," she said. "It sure is good to hear your voice. What's happening, girl?"

"Listen, I called because I have a big problem."

"And who am I—Dear Abby?" she asked.

"Listen, Bobby, I need someone with a brilliant brain to come up with a fantastic idea for me," I said.

"Well, then, you phoned the right person,"

she said. "Tell Aunty Bobby your problem, child."

I told her all the stuff about inventing a boyfriend. I have to admit I left out the part about using her name and showing her letters. I didn't quite know how she'd take that, and Bobby V. had a terrible temper. So I made it sound like I'd invented this boyfriend to get into a group where everyone else was in couples, and now I had to produce him at a dance. When I had finished, she did what I was sure she would do. She laughed. I had to hold the phone away from my ear because Bobby V. has a very loud laugh. In fact, when she used to laugh in school, everyone in the halls would turn around and stare.

"Well, it seems simple to me," she said when she had gotten her breath back. "All you have to do is find some guy to play the part of your boyfriend for the evening."

"And where do you think I'm going to find a fantastic actor who'd do that for me? I don't even *know* a single guy who could look like a cool motorcycle rider."

Bobby V. sighed. "You have a brother, dummy!"

"I can't use him to play my boyfriend," I said. "The kids all see him around here weekends."

"Not him, stupid, his friends," Bobby V. said, sighing again as if I were really dumb. "After all, Freddie must have friends, doesn't he? Ask him to lend you one of his friends for the evening."

That made me laugh because it was so impossible. "And why would he do that for me?" I asked.

"Tell him it's for a good cause."

"Very funny. You don't know my brother very well if you think he'd do anything for me."

"It's just a question of getting him at the right time," Bobby V. said. "Wait till he comes in after a date, when he's mellow, then play the poor little sister who needs her big brother's help. That always gets them."

"How would you know—you don't even have a big brother," I said. "Let me tell you that the only thing older brothers enjoy is teasing little sisters."

"Then you'll have to find something you can hold over him to make him help you. Snoop around a bit."

"Bobby V.—that's terrible. You mean black-mail?" I almost shrieked.

"If that's what you want to call it," she said calmly. "Personally, I call it persuasion."

"Bobby V., I *couldn't* do that. My brother

may tease me a lot, but as brothers go he's not too bad. I wouldn't snoop around or spy on him. I'll try and ask him on the weekend, but I'm not too hopeful."

After I had put the phone down, I began to think of ways I could appeal to my sweet, generous, loving older brother. But it all seemed rather hopeless. Freddie was not famous for being kind to his little sister. And even if he could be persuaded to help me, why should any of his friends do him a favor and take a skinny fifteen year old to a dance? I imagined telling Freddie. It made me go hot and cold all over just to think of it. He'd only laugh more than ever. He wouldn't understand at all. Worse still, he might tell Mom, and then I'd get in trouble at home.

"You were right, Grandma," I said out loud. "You do get punished for telling lies. I'm in trouble whatever happens. I might just as well own up to the kids and get it over with."

But I couldn't bring myself to confess just yet. Not, at least, until Freddie had come home for the weekend. I guess I was still hoping for a miracle to happen. Perhaps Freddie missed me now that he lived away from home. Perhaps he was lonely and would be only too glad to do his little sister a favor. Perhaps I could do something, like save his life, and in return he'd promise me anything I wanted.

"Hey, creep, how's it going? You better not have panty hose and makeup all over that bathroom!" Freddie greeted me at the front door. I guess that squashed any ideas about him missing me. He was still the same old mean Freddie.

"Hey, Mom, I'm home," he yelled. "Come and see who I've brought with me!"

My mother came running out into the hall, smoothing down her always smooth, wavy hair, a habit she had when visitors were around. Freddie opened the front door wider, and a tall, good-looking boy stepped inside.

"This is Flip Robertson, Mom," Freddie said. "His folks are away for the weekend, and I said he could come here—is that all right?"

Flip held out a hand to my mother, and I noticed the big gold ring on his pinkie. "I'm very glad to meet you, Mrs. Davis," he said. "And I want to let you know right now that I don't want to be a nuisance to you. But Freddie's been telling me all about your home cooking—"

"Well, isn't that nice," my mother said, smoothing down her hair again. I could tell she was flattered—she was very proud of her cooking. "We're happy to have you here, Flip. Freddie, you can put up the camp cot in your room for Flip. Candy, you can go and get some clean sheets out of the laundry closet. Candy! Did you hear me?"

"Oh—yes, Mom. Sure, Mom," I said, snapping back to reality. The wheels in my head had been working overtime. As soon as I saw Flip, I knew that he was just right for the part. He was tall and broad-shouldered, a really sharp dresser. His hair was slicked down smooth. His manner was self-assured, from the steady gaze of his almond-shaped eyes to the graceful way he walked. He was a perfect Bobby V.—he looked like a wild motorcycle rider. Now if I could only find some way to persuade him, to make him like me and want to help me out.

I gave him my biggest smile. "I'll go get the sheets for you, Flip, and I'll get my stuff out of your bathroom," I said sweetly as I walked away. When Freddie had brought the camp cot down from the attic, I helped make up the bed, tucking in the sheets and blankets neatly at the corners and smoothing down the pillow. I worked slowly, then hung around some more.

"It's OK, kid, you can get lost now," Freddie said in his usual gracious way.

"Oh, I thought maybe you would tell me about life in the big city," I said. "You know, what's happening at Lincoln High these days, how the basketball is going—"

"Not now. We've got some studying to do for a math test on Monday," Freddie said.

"I could help, I'm good at math," I said, and I smiled my best smile at Flip.

"I said get lost," Freddie threatened.

"Yeah—run along and play with your dollies or buy yourself an ice cream or whatever it is kids your age do," Flip said smoothly.

"I happen to be a high-school student just like you two," I said, trying to look mature and dignified. "So I guess I like to do the same sort of things you like to do."

"I hope not," Flip said to Freddie, with a knowing grin. "Man—I do hope not!"

As soon as I went out, they shut the door firmly behind me. Wow, I'd really made a hit there, I thought sarcastically. I really charmed Mr. Flip. He couldn't wait to get rid of me. Dollies indeed! Well, I guess that blew any chance I had of getting their help. I could never tell them now. All they'd do would be to laugh and act all superior. So Monday was the end of everything. On Monday I'd have to tell the kids at school, and then I wouldn't have any friends left.

Feeling really down, I decided to sit out on the patio to write a letter to Bobby V. That would make me feel better. I took a garden chair and an apple, setting up my chair in the shade. It was peaceful there. The only sounds came from far away—someone cutting a lawn down the block, little kids squealing in a paddling pool—happy sounds that belonged to the suburbs and not to the city, which made living in the suburbs so neat.

Dear Bobby V.,

Your great idea is just not going to work. My brother brought a friend home this weekend. The friend looks just right for the part, but there is no way I'm going to be able to get him to listen to me. They both treat me like a little kid and tell me to run away and play. To get Freddie to do anything for me, I'd have to rescue him from a burning building or something (and then, knowing Freddie, he'd probably say, "Thanks, creep, now get lost!").

So it looks as though by the time I write again I will have made a big fool of myself and be totally friendless.

I stopped, thinking over what I had just written. "Well, I guess it will serve me right," I scribbled after it. "I'm just not the type who can lie and get away with it. . . ."

I put my pen down and just listened to the suburban sounds for a moment. Then I became aware of Freddie and Flip's voices. Freddie's window was open, and they were sitting with their backs to it. They hadn't noticed me, sitting in the shade of the big plum tree. I couldn't help listening in. At first their conversation was boring. It really did seem that they were studying for a math test. It was so unheard-of for my brother to be studying anything that I guessed he must have been flunking math.

It was so nice there in the shade with a gentle breeze and the scent of spring flowers in the air that I closed my eyes and drifted off toward sleep. Then I heard something that made me open my eyes. I heard Flip say, in that bored sort of voice of his, "Man—do I have a whopper of a hangover!"

Freddie laughed. "Serves you right. I kept telling you to quit while you were ahead."

"Hey, listen," Flip said, "you were chug-a-lugging it pretty smooth, too."

"Well, I feel just fine," Freddie said. "But I

didn't drink nearly as many beers as you did. I was too busy trying to fight off Shirley."

Flip laughed. "You didn't look like you were fighting real hard to me."

"You're just jealous because Shirley was the foxiest lady in the place!"

"Me? Jealous? Hey, let me tell you, man—that Charlene was hot stuff, believe me."

"What time did you get home, anyway?"

"Home? Who went home?"

"Well, what did your folks say?"

"I told them I was spending the night with you, what else!"

Freddie burst out laughing. "That's great—I told the Joneses I was spending the night with *you*!"

They both roared with laughter.

I just sat there in the shade smiling quietly—like a cat with a big saucer of cream. All right, Freddie and Flip, I thought. That will teach you both to act like Mr. Big with me. Just one of those facts would have been enough for some gentle persuasion. With all of them together—I knew I'd just gotten me a dance partner!

Chapter Eight

I really couldn't believe my luck. I had not wanted to spy on my brother, I had never meant to spy on him. But now, without even trying, I had enough evidence to make him be my slave for the rest of his life. Of course, it wasn't going to be quite as easy as that. I mean, a shy, retiring girl like me can hardly go up to a six-foot basketball player with a mean temper and say, "Guess what I know about you?" Not if she's smart she won't!

No, one thing I was sure of—the time had to be just right. If I wanted Freddie and Flip to eat out of my hand, I had to make sure that the hand didn't get bitten off in the process.

I waited patiently all through dinner, thinking of what I wanted to say and how I was going to say it. But the golden opportunity never came up. Mom and Dad were right there all the time, listening to every word. We had hardly eaten the last spoonful of ice cream when Freddie jumped up.

"Thanks for dinner, Mom," he said. "See you later."

"Where are you going, Freddie?" my mother asked, sounding suspicious. When Freddie had lived at home, he had not been allowed to come and go as he pleased.

"Oh, just out—you know, driving around, showing Flip the highlights of Walnut Park by night," Freddie said vaguely. He knew how strict our parents could be. "We won't be late."

"Yeah, we just got to check out all those innocent, small-town girls, right, brother?" Flip butted in. I saw Freddie give him a dig in the ribs.

"Flip's just fooling around," Freddie said, giving him a very hard stare. Flip caught on.

"Oh, sure," he said, and gave a big, silly laugh. "We're just going cruising around, really. Maybe stop off and take in a movie or something."

"Well, you mind it is only a movie or something," my mother said pointedly. "My boy Freddie knows what I feel to be proper behavior. Right, Freddie?"

"Right, Mom," Freddie mumbled. "We'll be back soon. Don't worry. Come on, Flip."

I wanted to drop a hint right then that I knew, say something like "I know you two could do with an early night after last night," but they had gone before I'd even gotten up from the table.

I waited for them to come back, but I must have drifted off about eleven. The next thing I knew, the sun was streaming in my windows, and it was Sunday morning.

This is your last chance, I said to myself. It's now or never. You have a perfect opportunity. Don't blow it. I looked at my watch. Seven o'clock. I knew I had to act fast before Mom got up. She didn't sleep late, even on Sundays. I got out of bed and pulled on my robe. The whole house was silent, except for my father's snoring.

Right, Freddie, I thought. I'll get you while you're still half-asleep. That may be the best moment. All the same, I stood with my hand on Freddie's doorknob for a long while and took some deep breaths to calm myself before I got up the nerve to go in.

Freddie and Flip were still sprawled out, sound asleep. I stepped carefully around Flip and crept across to Freddie's bed. He was lying on his stomach with his pillow over his head. I moved the pillow away gently and tapped him on the shoulder.

"Freddie," I whispered into his ear.

"Wassamatter?" he mumbled.

"Freddie, it's me—Candy. I've got to talk to you!"

"Go away. I wantastayasleep!" he said, groaning. He pulled the pillow back over his head.

I removed it, firmly this time. "Yes, now," I hissed in his ear. "I have to talk to you before Mom and Dad wake up."

Freddie turned onto his back and opened one eye a fraction of an inch to look at his clock. "You crazy, girl?" he asked quite clearly this time. "It's Sunday morning. Why would I want to talk to you at seven o'clock on Sunday morning?"

"It's something important," I whispered. "Something we don't want Mom to know."

"Look, kid," he said, "save your little secrets for the little kids at your school, OK? And let me get some sleep!! I don't even want to talk to you when I'm awake, and right now I am definitely still asleep." He pulled the covers over his head again, turned over, and groaned.

"Poor Freddie," I said. "Don't tell me you

have a hangover again! Not like the one you and Flip got the night after that party!"

Freddie rolled over, and both his eyes shot wide open.

"What did you say?" he asked.

"I was just reminding you about the party," I said, trying to sound calm, though I was petrified. Now that I'd gone this far I couldn't back out, however mad Freddie got at me. "You know—the party when everyone thought you were spending the night at Flip's house and Flip's folks thought he was here?"

Freddie leaped out of bed, hurdled over the sleeping Flip, and shut the door. "Not so loud," he said. "You want Mom to hear?"

"Of course I don't want Mom and Dad to hear," I said. "I wouldn't want them to know about *any* of the *things* that went on at that party."

"How did you know about that party?" Freddie demanded. "Who told you?"

"Nobody told me. I just happened to be doing my homework in the backyard yesterday, and your window just happened to be open, so I couldn't help hearing every word you both said. Boy, were you lucky that Mom wasn't weeding the flower bed out there!"

"Right on to that," he said. "I don't know what she'd do if she found out. She'd make me come and live with her again and never let me out of her sight. It would be terrible. Listen, Candy—you weren't thinking of telling Mom and Dad, were you?"

"Who, me?" I asked.

"Yeah, I mean—us kids have got to stick together, right? You wouldn't tell on your own brother!"

"What do you take me for?" I asked sweetly. "My lips are sealed."

"That's my girl," he said. "I always knew you would grow up all right."

"Of course, there is one small favor I want to ask in return," I said slowly.

"I knew it." Freddie sighed. "I knew there had to be a good reason for waking me in the middle of the night. You want money, right?"

"Wrong."

"Well, what do you want?"

"It's only a very small favor, Freddie. I want you to loan me Flip for an evening."

"You want what?"

"Flip."

"Flip?" he said loudly. Flip heard his name, turned over, and mumbled something in his sleep. Freddie lowered his voice again. "What do you want Flip for? He's not your type. He's certainly not the type of guy I'd trust with my little sister."

"I don't want to date him, Freddie," I said. "At least, I want him to be my date but not like you think. It's hard to explain."

"Try me," he said.

I took a deep breath and began. "Well, basically, I've been asked to bring a boy to a dance. That boy doesn't exist. I made him up. I know it was dumb, but it just sort of happened. Now I have to bring him to the dance, or I'll look like a fool, and I won't have any friends."

"What sort of friends are they if they'd drop you because you didn't have a boyfriend?" he asked, bringing up the question that had been nagging at me all along.

"Well, they're the only friends I've got," I said. "You don't know how it is in a small school. If Helen and Diana don't like me, I'll never have friends."

"I understand, I think," Freddie said. "It's tough, changing schools in the middle of a year. But this thing with Flip—you want him to act the part of your boyfriend—is that it?"

"Right."

Freddie laughed. "You're crazy," he said. "You don't know Flip. He has enough girls hanging around him never to need extra ones. There's no way I could persuade him to do a crazy thing like that."

"So his folks aren't very strict with him, then?" I asked. "They don't care much what he does?"

"Flip's folks?" Freddie said. "Why, his old man takes a stick to him!"

"Then he'll do it," I said. "After all, I managed to persuade you, didn't I? A night at a dance with me must be a whole lot better than a whipping."

Freddie looked at me, and his face broke into a grin. "I don't know," he said slowly. "If it were me, it'd be a hard choice!"

Then I hit him and woke up Flip.

Chapter Nine

Two Saturdays before the dance Ginger and I went shopping for dresses. She was turning out to be a good friend, and she was really easy to get along with. I couldn't believe my good luck in finding someone like her right next door.

I had been worrying about a dress for the dance because I didn't have anything that was right, and I was scared that my mother might offer to make one for me. My mother tried hard, but she was no good at sewing, and anything she made looked as if it was designed for an older sister who weighed a hundred pounds more than I did. The problem was, I had only a little money in my bank account, and I didn't want to ask my folks for any after all the expenses of the move.

But then Ginger popped into volleyball practice one night. I caught sight of her freckled face smiling down at me from the bleachers.

"What are you doing here?" I asked as soon as Jonathan had let us go. "Don't you have enough violence to watch on TV?"

She laughed and came bounding down the bleachers. "I thought I had better come and see the new superjock for myself," she said.

"You don't mean me," I said. "You're joking."

"No, I'm not. You look terrific," she said. "The kids are all talking about you."

"Which kids?"

"I have my spies. By the way, one of my spies says you're bringing a real hunk from out of town to the dance. Is that right?"

"Sort of," I murmured. I hated to lie to Ginger. I changed the subject hastily. "Are you coming?"

Her face lit up. "You bet. And you'll never guess who I'm bringing."

"Not Brent Holmes from the chess club?"

"The very same."

"But I thought he never said anything to you except checkmate?"

"He didn't. But one day I couldn't stand it any longer, and I said, 'How about coming to the Spirit Week Dance with me?' and he said OK."

"That's great, Ginger."

"Then he said checkmate," she said and giggled.

As we walked home together, she said, "You know, Candy, I've been meaning to ask you— do you ever do any baby-sitting?"

"I used to sometimes. I'd like to, I could sure use the money."

"That's great," she said, "because I've got more than I can handle just now. Since Mom's gone back to work, I have to help with dinner and the house, and there just doesn't seem to be the time. How about if I introduce you to some of the families I usually sit for?"

"Gee, thanks, Ginger," I said. "You've saved my life. I needed a dress for the dance so badly, and I was scared my mother would make me one. You haven't seen her sewing. I didn't want to ask them for the money, but I wouldn't mind asking them to loan it to me until I can pay it back from baby-sitting."

"I need a dress too," Ginger said. "You want to come shopping on Saturday?"

So on Saturday morning Ginger took me around to all the good shops in Walnut Park. We found a dress for her pretty quickly—a sort of prairie dress in a pretty cotton print with big puffy sleeves and lots of lace. It was just right on her. In fact she looked like she'd just left her covered wagon outside. I tried on some similar dresses, but they weren't right for me. I'm just not the lace-and-frills type. By the end of the morning I found out that I was not the slinky-satin type either. I tried on a red satin dress, and Ginger and I had a good laugh over it.

Then in the one big department store Ginger found the perfect dress.

"Hey, Candy," she called, "get over here. This one is just right."

And it was. It was a long dress in pale ice blue made of a fabric that shimmered as I moved. It fitted me perfectly—nice and snug around the curves and then swirling out into a full skirt. It was the sort of dream dress you never think you'll own.

When I saw the price, I *knew* it was a dream dress. "What a bummer," I said. "I can't afford a dress like this, even with baby-sitting."

We didn't find anything else I liked, and I walked home feeling very down. Though my mother promised to drive me into the big regional shopping center a few miles away, I still felt sad about that dress.

Then the following Wednesday, the impossible happened. Ginger came bursting into our house, so out of breath that she could hardly talk. "You'll never believe it," she said panting. 'Your dress!! They've got your dress on sale! I was just there, and it's been marked down!"

We rushed back to the store, and there it was. I could hardly believe my luck. As I got out the money to pay for it, I kept expecting the saleslady to say, "There is a mistake. This dress was not supposed to be reduced." But she didn't. I almost ran out of the store before she could change her mind.

"Somebody up there must like me," I told Ginger when we were safely on the sidewalk, my dress wrapped in delicate pink tissue paper inside a big silver box.

Finally the night of the dance came, and I didn't know whether to feel scared or excited. I had never been to a real dance before—not a high-school dance with pretty dresses and guys in suits and a real band. My mother was as excited as I was, and she helped me get ready.

"Why, I think it's so nice of Flip to take you to the dance," she kept on saying. "What a kind thing to do. He must remember what it feels like to be young and shy and not have a partner. Of course, your brother must have given him the idea. He's such a good boy, your brother Freddie. There aren't many brothers who would look after their sisters that way."

I looked at my shoes and didn't say anything. My mouth kept wanting to twitch into a silly grin. My mother fussed around me like an old hen all the time I was getting ready. I suppose she was finally enjoying having a daughter. I had been such a shy kid until then that she hadn't had much practice. Frankly, I wished she would go away and let me get dressed alone. She didn't have a clue about what girls should look like these days, and it was hard to look how I wanted to look and not be rude to her at the same time. I knew she meant well, but she was sure testing my patience!

"Here, Candy," she called, trotting into the room with her latest treasure. "Why don't you take this shawl to drape around your shoulders? It gets pretty cold by midnight." And she handed me a terrible-looking thing with big red flowers and a fringe around it.

"Er—no thanks, Mom. I'll be so excited I won't get cold—and I'd only leave it somewhere," I said.

"Then what about this necklace? That would look pretty with your blue dress."

"Oh no, Mom. I couldn't. I'd be scared I'd

break it or lose it or something. I'm just fine as I am, really."

"You sure are, honey," she said, looking me up and down, a satisfied expression on her face.

After she had gone, I took a long hard look at myself in the mirror. "Candy Davis," I said to my reflection, "you don't look half bad. Who would have thought it!" The girl in the mirror looked back at me with very bright, shining eyes. She looked so pretty I could hardly believe it was me. The tiny blue flowers I had stuck into my dark curls just matched the color of my dress. And the dress fitted me so well. Almost as if it had been made specially for me. I had worried about fitting into the tight top but—another miracle—I wasn't quite so straight-up-and-down as I had been. I curved exactly where the dress curved.

I'm finally beginning to look the way a girl is supposed to, I said to myself. Maybe Flip won't mind taking me to the dance as much as he thought. If I was a boy, I wouldn't mind being seen with me!

Then a little thought flashed across my mind before I could stop it. I wonder if Jonathan will be there? I wonder what he'll think of me tonight?

I was right about Flip. He did a double take when I walked into the living room. "Hey—" he said slowly, looking me up and down as if I were a model in a display case. "Hey—little sister is growing up. I don't think Fearless Freddie would trust me with you if he saw you looking like that!"

"Have a good time," my mother called as we walked toward Flip's old Chevy. It was the sort of car you didn't see around much any-more—you know, the kind that has fins and snarls at you! But it still ran, and it was better than walking or having my father drive me.

"Take good care of my little girl!" my father called down the path. He made it sound like a threat.

"Don't worry, Dad," I called back. Nothing in the world was going to stop me from hav-ing a good time that night. I was going to my first real dance with a great-looking guy.

This is it, I thought. This is what being a teenager is all about and what high school should be like. I grinned happily to myself, then stole a quick glance at Flip. He looked just right for the part he was going to play. By strange coincidence he was wearing a light blue suit that matched my dress perfectly. His hair was slicked down into neat little waves, and his mouth was curved into a little secret smile.

Me and Bobby V., I thought happily. I can't wait till Diana sees this!

Flip must have sensed me looking at him. He turned and smiled at me, flashing all those perfect white teeth. "Just you and me, baby, right?" he said. "I'm going to show you one good time tonight!"

The moment he pulled into the high-school parking lot was worth everything. It was worth all those nights I worried about the lie I'd told. In fact, watching Diana's face alone was worth anything, even the terrible punishment my grandma said would happen to me.

We had arranged to meet outside the gym at nine o'clock. It was ten after by the time we arrived, and I wondered for a moment whether they had gone in without us. But then I saw them standing in the shadows beside the gym door—waiting for us.

"Come on, let's go meet the gang, *Bobby V.*," I said, and I took Flip's hand.

George was in the middle of a funny story, as usual. He broke off when he caught sight of us. One by one all the kids turned around until all their eyes were on us. I felt my cheeks burning, but this was my big moment, and I was not going to blow it.

"Hi, everyone," I said brightly. "Sorry we're a bit late, but Bobby V. here got caught up in traffic driving out from the city."

I saw their eyes all swing to my partner, and I could tell they were impressed.

"So this is Bobby V.," Helen said. "We've all been dying to meet you."

Diana slunk over to him. Slunk is really the only word to describe the way she moved. She was wearing a tight red Hawaiian print dress, and she moved like a snake in it. "Hi," she said in her deep, soft voice. "I'm Diana. We were getting worried that you didn't exist."

I saw Flip's eyes open wide, and I was suddenly terrified that I'd lost my date before the evening even started.

"Well, hi there, Diana," Flip said smoothly. "Are you convinced now that I exist?"

She laughed, a deep throaty laugh. "Oh, yeah. You exist all right. I can tell you're all flesh and blood." She was now standing inches away from him.

"Where's your motorcycle?" she asked. "Because I am dying to take a ride on it."

"My what?" Flip asked.

I'd been thinking about how to get him away from Diana, wondering if I should remind him tactfully about his strict father and about sticking to deals. Now I woke up to the more immediate danger—that Flip might say the wrong thing and blow my whole story.

"Your bike, Bobby!" I interrupted. "Diana wanted a ride on your bike. Too bad we came in your brother's car tonight."

Flip grinned as if he caught on. "Oh, that bike," he said. "Sorry—I didn't bring my bike tonight. You can't take a girl to a dance on a bike!"

"What a bummer," Diana said, fluttering her eyelashes at him. "I'd always wanted a ride on a big, powerful motorcycle—you know, go racing through the darkness with my dress streaming out in the wind."

"Yeah, and get it caught in the back wheel and kill both of you," George said dryly. The other kids laughed, and the tension was broken.

"Let's go in, you guys," Helen said. "I'm getting cold out here, and besides, we're missing out on that good music." As we turned to go, she grabbed my arm. "He is awesome, Candy," she whispered. "You're a lucky girl."

Flip took hold of my arm, and I floated into the gym. I didn't care that my date was here only because of a lie and some blackmail. I was with a total hunk—the cutest guy at the dance, and I felt like a million dollars.

Diana was my only real worry, but it turned

out that she was more interested in the motorcycle than the boy because she hardly bugged Flip after we started dancing. And Flip was a perfect partner. During one of the first dances, he looked across at Diana's swaying back. "That's quite a girl," he said. Then he must have noticed the worry in my face because he added quickly, "But let me tell you right now, baby—I am not the kind of guy who changes partners in the middle of the evening. When I come with a girl, I stick with her!" Then he gave me his wonderful, flashing smile, and I felt like a million dollars again.

Flip not only looked good, he danced like a dream. He knew all the latest dance steps and made me try them all. Maybe some of his smoothness rubbed off on me or something, but soon I began to feel less and less shy. After a while I noticed that other couples had stopped dancing just to watch us. In the slow numbers he held me real tight. In fact the evening was passing by in such a sweet, romantic dream that I was not prepared for a couple of shocks.

The first shock came when Ginger danced up to us. "Hi, Candy," she called. "Are you having fun?" Then she noticed my partner. "Hey, isn't that your brother's friend—" she blurted out. I remembered that she had seen him when he was staying for the weekend with Freddie. Of course Diana and her partner had to be right bebind us at that moment, ready to hear every word.

"That's right," I said loudly and quickly before she could say anything else. "This is Bobby V. from the city. Remember I told you all about him?"

She must have noticed that I was acting weirdly. "Oh, yes," she said. "Bobby V. Sure—I remember now."

Then she danced away again.

The other shock came later in the evening.

"I have to go freshen up," Helen said. "You coming to the powder room, Candy?"

"Sure," I said, "although that's a fancy name to give to the girls' locker room!" We laughed and got up from our table.

"Don't dance with anyone while we're gone!" Helen called back to the boys. We fought our way across the floor filled with wildly dancing couples. Helen, who is a lot more pushy than I, managed to get us across safely. On the way back she went ahead of me, and I was trapped in the middle of violently waving arms and shaking bodies. Suddenly I looked up at the figure in front of me—it was Jonathan. His face lit up when he saw me, and I was not prepared for the strange wave of emotion that went through me—pleasure at seeing him unexpectedly mixed with embarrassment about seeing him in the wrong setting and at the wrong time.

"Oh, hi, Candy," he yelled above the throbbing music. "I was wondering if you'd come tonight. I don't usually come to these things, but I thought—"

He broke off. The other dancers had pushed us very close together. "You look very nice tonight," he said. "Very grown up. Will you dance with me?"

"I'd like to, Jonathan, but not right now," I stammered. "You see I—"

Just at that moment the music stopped, and the dancers began to trickle off the dance floor. The band put down their instruments and got up from the stage.

"How about that," Jonathan said. He laughed, a little uneasily. "I ask a young lady to dance with me, and then the band leaves. Is that fair?"

I smiled. "They'll be back," I said.

"Will you dance with me then?" he asked. He looked so unsure of himself, so different from the bully who yelled at me. Now there was something about him like a little lost boy—it made him very appealing.

"Maybe later," I said hesitantly. "I'd really like to, but—"

I was about to say yes. I wanted to say yes, but then I heard a voice loudly calling my name. "Hey, Candy! What are you doing? Get over here—I'm getting lonely sitting here all by myself!"

Jonathan and I both looked toward Flip.

"Oh, I'm sorry," Jonathan mumbled. "I didn't realize you were here with a date. I hope I haven't embarrassed you." And before I could say anything, he had melted into the darkness at the side of the stage. I stood there looking after him for quite a while before I went back to Flip.

Well, it's only for tonight, I thought. Flip isn't really my date. I've got to remember that. After tonight I'll never see him again, probably.

But even as I was having that thought, I felt confused and a little sad. After all, Flip was a terrific date, and I could see that everyone admired him and envied me for being with him. That was quite a new sensation—to have other girls envy me! I was pretty sure that never again in my life would I have such a smooth, great-looking boy as my date.

After the dance, Flip glided the car to a halt outside my house.

"Thank you, Flip," I said. "I had a wonderful time. That was the best night of my whole life."

"That's me, good old Mr. Kindness himself," Flip said jokingly. "Always willing to come to the rescue of poor lost girls." Then he smiled at me. "I'll let you into a little secret if you promise not to tell Freddie—I had a pretty good time myself. You kids out here know how to enjoy yourselves—and you, you were a good partner."

"Thanks," I said, beaming at him. I opened the door to get out.

His hand reached out and grabbed my wrist. "Hey, wait a minute," he said. "Who said the date was over yet? What's supposed to happen at the end of dates? Come here." He pulled me toward him, and before I knew what was happening, he was kissing me.

I had often imagined my first kiss. I'd even practiced puckering up in front of the mirror so that I wouldn't be too bad at it. But I'd always secretly thought that it might be pretty embarrassing, with me and the boy bumping noses or not knowing what to do. But I had never imagined my first with someone like Flip. He knew just what to do. He had obviously had lots of practice, and there was no nose bumping or anything else wrong. It was just perfect—the sort of kiss you see in the movies; the sort of kiss where your whole body melts and floats away until you are no longer part of the real world.

I didn't want it to stop ever. But it did. Suddenly our front door opened, and light streamed into the car. We both sat up suddenly and guiltily. My father was standing at the front door. He came down the path toward us.

"Your mother thought she heard a car stop," he said as he opened the car door.

Flip smiled at me, reached out, and patted my hand. "Good night, kid," he said. "See ya around."

As I climbed out of the car and walked with my father toward the house, I replayed that phrase over and over in my mind. "See ya around," he had said. Did he really mean it?

Chapter Ten

The next day I knew exactly how Cinderella felt after the ball. I looked at myself in the mirror and wondered, Did that really happen to me? And, like Cinderella, I wondered, Will I ever see him again? I had to keep taking a peek at that dress hanging in my closet to remind myself that it hadn't all been a dream. I tried to get all my feelings down when I wrote to Bobby V. "It almost seems too good to be true," I wrote. "Flip looked so handsome, and I could see all the other girls were jealous. Can you imagine other girls being jealous of *me*? I felt so grown up. At the end of the evening, after he had kissed me good night (and that was fantastically, wonderfully dreamy, too), he said he'd see me again—at least I think he said it. I know I'm going to be a bundle of nerves waiting for the phone to ring. . . .”

Then life went back to normal, and I didn't have much time for daydreaming because volleyball started to take all my energy and attention. The first game of the season was coming up—against El Camino High, our biggest rival.

I had never expected to make first team, but when the list was put up on the sports notice board, I saw my name on it. And for someone who had never cared about sports before, I felt stupidly happy and proud. I couldn't wait for Freddie to get home on the weekend to tell him he wasn't the only superjock in the family!

But being on first team did have its drawbacks. If I'd thought we worked out hard before, I was wrong. Jonathan now started us on a routine of fitness training that left each of us crawling off the court almost half-dead.

“Hear the rumor that's going around?” Helen said after one practice as we thirstily gulped down water. “This rumor is that he's got one person too many on the squad, and he's not sure who to drop—so he's going to keep this up until one of us drops dead!”

"I see," Sharron said. "The person who drops dead first is cut!"

"That figures," I added. "And I have a suspicion the person he's after is me."

"Why do you say that?" Helen asked, wiping drops of water from her chin. "You're one of our best players. He wouldn't want to get rid of you."

"Then why is he picking on me?" I asked.

"He wants you to be even better, I guess," Helen said and walked off to take a shower. I followed her. In my own shower I couldn't help thinking about Jonathan. Actually, I didn't want to think about him because he made me confused. To start with, I thought he liked me, then he hated me, then he was definitely getting to like me again, and at the dance it almost seemed that—well, let's just say that he didn't look at me like a volleyball coach looks at a player. But now, after the dance, he was back to his mean old self. When he wasn't shouting at me, he ignored me. After practice if we all went off for a soda, he walked in the other direction. It was like trying to understand Dr. Jekyll and Mr. Hyde.

"What makes him so moody?" I asked when we were getting dressed. "Has he always been like that?"

"He's always been sort of distant," Helen

said. "You never really get to know him. But I have to say that he's gotten much meaner since you arrived."

"I didn't realize I had that effect on people," I said. "Perhaps he couldn't bear to watch as bad a volleyball player as me."

"But you're good now, and he's still mean," one of the other girls added.

"Maybe he's having girlfriend trouble," another girl suggested. But when we talked about it, it seemed that nobody knew who his girlfriend was or whether he even had one this year.

"He didn't bring anyone to the dance," someone remarked. "And I know he took a girl to the junior prom last spring."

I had decided not to think about Jonathan. His girlfriend problems only concerned me when he yelled at me in practice—and besides, I was using all my spare time dreaming about Flip. I had this nicely planned daydream all figured out. I would be sitting doing nothing one evening, and the telephone would ring. It would be Flip. . . .

"Candy," he would say, "I tried going back to my mature parties and mature girlfriends, but it wasn't any good. I could only think about you. I just have to see you again—and soon."

This was a very nice daydream, but unfortunately it remained just a daydream. Every evening I waited by the phone. Every time the phone rang I held my breath, but it was always someone else.

One night Ginger was at my place. She had taken to stopping by after she'd finished her chores so we could do our homework together. She was not too great at math, but I found it easy, and I was not too great at social studies, but she was a whiz there, so we made a good team.

"Candy, is something bothering you?" she asked suddenly.

"Bothering me?" I said innocently. "Why do you ask?"

"Because you keep jumping up and down like a jack-in-the-box and because you've written eleven times seven is two hundred and eighteen."

"Oh," I said, "I guess I'm not concentrating well tonight."

"Must be some guy," she said knowingly.

I didn't argue.

Then the phone rang. "I'll get it!" I yelled and cleared the entire room in two leaps.

"Hello," I said panting, "yes—this is Candy. Oh—Hi, Sharron. Yes, I do have it. It's pages eighty-seven through ninety-five. You're welcome. Bye."

I put the phone back. "That was Sharron," I said. "She wanted the biology assignment."

Ginger smiled. "It doesn't take Sherlock Holmes to deduce that you're waiting for a guy to call you," she said. "Is it someone I know?"

"You saw him at the dance."

"Oh, him," she said. "He looks so mature. Is he a senior or something? I saw him once at your house, didn't I? I thought he was Freddie's friend."

"He was," I said. "But I sort of borrowed him."

"Cute guy," she said, a little hesitantly I thought. "Did he say he'd call you?"

"More or less, but now I'm not so sure."

"Don't worry about it," Ginger said kindly. "I always think it's fate. If you two are destined to be together, he'll call you. But somehow I always thought that you and Jonathan. . . ." Her voice trailed off, and she took a long sip of Coke.

As the days passed, I began to lose hope. If Flip really did want to see me again, he would have called by now. In fact, I knew all along it was pretty hopeless. Flip had only done what he'd promised. He had given a poor little nobody freshman a good time. Mr. Kindness, he had called himself. Now he was probably making jokes about it to his friends at wild parties. Even the kiss in the car probably meant nothing to him. He probably kissed every girl he went with, just for practice.

I made myself stop thinking about him, but I couldn't stop him from creeping into my dreams at night. Except for the night before the volleyball game. I was so nervous that I couldn't get to sleep until two, and when I finally did fall asleep, my dreams were so full of missed shots and yelling Jonathans that I woke up sweating, hardly daring to fall asleep again.

In the morning I woke up feeling terrible. My head was pounding, and my stomach was in such a tight knot that I couldn't manage to swallow a spoonful of my Wheaties.

"You won't be any use out there if you don't eat," my father coaxed. "Freddie always eats a huge breakfast before a game."

"But I can't make myself eat. I'm too nervous," I said.

"It's only a game, honey," my mother said soothingly. "No cause to get yourself into a state over a game. It doesn't really matter who wins as long as you have a good time."

"You try telling that to Jonathan," I said. "He doesn't yell at *you*!"

Somehow I got through the day at school, but I still wasn't feeling any better as I changed into my uniform in the locker room. The other girls seemed just as nervous as I was.

"Have you seen their players yet?" Crissy whispered as she grabbed my arm. "I used to think you were tall, but they're all *giants*. It's just not *fair*. I bet they're all boys in disguise!"

"They should make a height limit," another girl said.

"Or feed Candy her spinach so that she can catch up with them," someone else quipped.

"Or put Jonathan in a uniform and send him out to play for us!"

"Yeah—and make him do those dives he makes us do."

"And yell if he doesn't do them right."

"I bet he can't even do them. He probably can't even play the game at all!"

By now we were all laughing and shouting, and we felt a lot better as we walked out to warm up. The Camino girls were certainly big. They hit very hard—I know because I took one of their spikes on my thigh, which was tender for weeks. But two things they didn't do very well—they didn't move quickly, and they were scared to dive for a low ball.

That was where all our bruises paid off and where short girls like Helen had an advantage. Helen seemed to be everywhere, diving under people's feet and saving impossible shots. When my turn came to be up at the net, I suddenly seemed to have grown taller. My arms seemed a lot longer, too. I jumped up high and reached out sideways. They couldn't get anything past me. And we *won!*

When it was all over, I overheard one of their girls say to another, "We would have been all right if only we could have gotten something past that octopus at the net." And for the first time I didn't take it as an insult. For the first time in my life being a bean pole with long arms had paid off!

We were a pretty rowdy bunch of girls as we left the locker room. Only Jonathan was strangely quiet and withdrawn.

"Well, coach," Helen asked jokingly, "are you satisifed with us now, or will you keep on driving us to exhaustion?"

He smiled and put his arm around her shoulder. "You did a good job, kid. I'm proud of all of you." His eyes came to rest on me. "And you—Candy—you were fantastic," he said. "I knew you could do it. The first time I saw you, I knew you could make a fine player. You worked hard, and you deserved to win."

"Thanks, Jonathan," I muttered, feeling shy and awkward and still not sure what to do about compliments.

"Hey, everyone, why don't we all go home and get changed and then meet for pizza?" someone suggested.

"Great idea!" all the other voices answered.

"You coming, Jonathan?" Helen asked.

"Wouldn't miss it," he said.

Then I remembered what day it was. We were going to have dinner with my grandmother, and that was something I couldn't and didn't want to get out of.

"I'm sorry, I can't come," I said. "I have to go into the city this evening."

Somehow my eyes drifted to Jonathan's face. "Oh, of course, we forgot," he said coldly. "Candy has a prior engagement as usual." Then he stalked away.

As I watched his back I finally began to understand—Jonathan was jealous! He thought my prior engagement was a date with Flip, and he was jealous!

Chapter Eleven

The nice thing about my grandmother's house was that it never changed. Every time you walked up the front steps you smelled the star jasmine, which curled up the white lattice. It was like stepping back into a warm, safe memory of childhood. Everything was just as I remembered it—the tiny living room, right inside the front door, smelling of polish and crowded with old, heavy furniture that was too big for the room. The table was usually covered with a fringed tablecloth, under which I'd played house as a little girl. Every surface was crowded with old photographs— wedding pictures, Grandma as a little girl in a white frilly dress with her hair tied in a lot of little pigtails, relatives in uniforms from several different wars, Freddie and me as babies, me as a second-grader with no front teeth—a whole family history piled onto the piano and various tables.

And Grandma herself never seemed to change, either. She had always been small and shrunken—a little doll of a woman to fit her miniature dollhouse. But this time she looked, if anything, even a little smaller and frailer.

"Just let me take a good look at you, Candy child," she said as she hugged me with a strength you would never have suspected she had. "Grown another inch since I saw you last, I do declare."

"I can't help it, Grandma," I said.

"Well, you better stop it pretty soon, or you won't find yourself a husband," she said.

I laughed, and she looked at me carefully. "But I must say, I reckon you've grown prettier, too! You're beginning to look like a young lady. And about time. Maybe you will find yourself a husband after all."

"I've got news for you, Grandma," I said. "Finding a husband isn't the only thing in a girl's life anymore. We have careers, too, these days."

"That's what they all say, until they get scared they are going to end up as old maids!" my grandma said laughing. "Then they jump

107

at the first man they see. But I can't stand here talking all night," she said, hurrying into the kitchen. "I'll be letting the pies burn, and everyone knows you only come for my good homemade pies!"

I smiled happily as she went. She seemed to have gotten back some of her old fighting spirit, which she'd lost when Auntie Marleen had looked after her.

We were just sitting down to dinner when Freddie arrived.

"I smelled that pie baking a block away," he called, kissing Grandma on the cheek and grabbing himself a piece of chicken all in one movement. "By the way," he mumbled to me with his mouth full, "I got a message for you from somebody."

"Who?"

"Tell you later," he said, piling mashed potatoes on his plate and leaving me guessing. Could it be a message from Flip?

I waited impatiently all evening, but it wasn't until we were walking out to the car that he grabbed my arm and drew me back. "That crazy guy Flip!" he whispered. "He's gone clean out of his mind."

"What's he done?" I asked.

"He asked me to give you a message, that's what," Freddie said. "I told him he needs his head examined, but he wants to take you on a date!"

That night I could hardly sleep, I was so excited.

How about that, I thought. Daydreams really do come true. Me, little old Candy Davis, who was so boring that nobody ever looked at her twice—and suddenly in one day one cute senior wants to date me, and another cute senior gets jealous because I don't go for pizza with him. It's all too good to be true. I really don't think I can stand this pace for long!

I had several bad moments during the next week when I decided that the whole thing had been a cruel joke between Freddie and Flip. I convinced myself that Flip hadn't really asked me for a date at all. I'd get ready and he wouldn't show up and later they'd both laugh about it. After all, why hadn't he telephoned me himself? He was certainly not the shy type.

The evening of the date I took a long time to get ready. I went through my entire closet again and again, but nothing seemed quite right to wear with Flip. My skirts and dresses all seemed too little-girlish. I could imagine meeting Flip's friends and hearing them make jokes about cradle-snatching. Let's face it, I thought gloomily. I just don't have any sexy outfits—and even if I did, they wouldn't look right on me. I am no Diana, and I never will be.

In the end I played it safe and wore jeans. After all, I wasn't quite sure where we were going, and jeans are OK most places—unless he decided to take me to the opera or a French restaurant, neither of which was likely! I had a new pair of white denims, which I'd only worn once, and a very pale lilac blouse with a high neck and puffy sleeves. It was an old-fashioned sort of blouse, more frilly than I usually wore, but it looked right on me. When I was all dressed, I felt quite pleased with the way I looked. I passed the time until Flip arrived by experimenting with nail polish.

My nails had dried, and I glanced up at the clock. It was past eight-thirty and no sign of Flip. I felt panic rising again—had my fears been right? Was he really not coming? Freddie hadn't mentioned a time, but surely you came to take a girl on a date before nine o'clock, especially when that girl's parents were strict about her getting home before midnight. I paced my room while a whole jumble of thoughts danced around in my brain. There's nothing I can do but wait—I could call him! No, that wouldn't do at all. What if he didn't even know about the evening? What if it was only Freddie's idea of a joke, and he hadn't even told Flip? No, phoning was definitely out.

Will you sit down and relax? Put on a record, read a book, anything to stop this pacing up and down. What does it matter if he doesn't come? He's nothing to me. Only one boy—there are millions more in the world. He wasn't my type anyway. He would have found me boring. . . .

The clock in the living room chimed nine. Nine slow bongs. Please come, Flip, I pleaded, then turned it into a prayer. Please let him come—I don't want to look like a fool sitting here all dressed up for nothing.

I tried to read, tried to sit down, but it was no good. I heard the clock chime nine-fifteen and then nine-thirty. By then I was convinced that he wasn't coming. There never had been a date with Flip—it was all a cruel joke. I've even done my nails for nothing, I thought, which shows you how emotionally upset I was by that time!

When the doorbell rang at nine-forty, I didn't even open my door to find out who it was. It would only be someone for Mom, and then I would be doubly disappointed.

Then I heard Dad calling my name. "There's

a young man here waiting for you, Candy," he called. "Are you ready yet?"

I longed to go over and hug my dad. He knew I had been ready and waiting for hours, but he wasn't going to give me away. I came out, and there was Flip, looking as cool and handsome as ever, smiling at me with his wonderful smile that made my knees go all weak.

"Don't worry, Mr. Davis," he called to my father. "She's in good hands."

"Don't keep her out too late," my father said as he shut the front door.

"Where are we going?" I asked as I climbed into his car. "Isn't it a bit late to go out?"

Flip laughed. "Where have you been all your life?" he asked. "Don't you know that no party ever starts before ten or eleven? That is, no *fun* party!"

"That's usually the time I have to be home," I said. "I guess I haven't led your kind of life."

"Don't worry about it, baby," he said. "You got a lot of growing up to do. But you stick with old Flip, and he'll show you how to have a good time!"

Then he put his foot down on the gas, and we roared off into the night.

As we moved onto the freeway, his arm

slipped around my shoulder, and he drew me toward him. "Hey, baby," he whispered, "how about a little kiss?"

"Flip, we're on a freeway. You need to watch the road!" I said, anxiously watching all the other cars.

He laughed. "I've got this old car so well trained, I just say 'Home,' and it goes there without me driving it," he said. He put his foot down and moved out into the fast lane.

"Flip, I'd be happier if you had two hands on the wheel when you're going fast like this," I pleaded.

"Hey, come on, relax, will you?" he crooned. "You call this fast? I'll show you fast." The car seemed to jerk forward and sprang away like an eager racehorse from the starting gate. We flashed past other cars. I watched the needle creep up and up until I was too scared to say anything. I knew if I complained, he'd only show off more.

Just when I was feeling so scared I thought I'd throw up, I saw the red light shining through the rear window.

"Flip, it's the police," I said, grabbing his arm.

"Don't worry, we'll soon get rid of them," he said, slowing down and pulling over smoothly. "Don't you say a word, and we'll be out of here in no time, understand?"

I nodded. How could I say a word when I was too scared to open my mouth? Flip didn't seem scared at all. He wound down the window as a big policeman strolled up to us.

"You were going rather fast back there, weren't you?" the policeman said. "Let me see your license."

Flip handed it over. "Sorry, officer," he said smoothly. "I know I was speeding, but I was kind of worried about my girl here. She's not feeling too good, and I wanted to get her home in a hurry."

"What's the problem, miss?" the policeman asked, turning to me.

"She ate something that didn't agree with her, and she feels pretty sick," Flip answered for me. "I couldn't stop on the freeway, and I didn't want her to throw up all over my upholstery."

The cop turned back to me. He looked concerned, and I felt terrible. "Will you be OK, young lady?"

I nodded. The policeman smiled. "All right. I'll let you off this time. You get her home as quickly as possible, but don't let me catch you going over the limit again."

"Oh, you won't, officer," Flip said. Then as we pulled off the shoulder, he added, "I'll be going so fast you'll never catch me next time," and he burst out laughing.

"Man, did we fool him," he yelled. "Those dumb cops are so easy to fool. Did I or did I not make a jackass out of him!"

Chapter Twelve

By the time we arrived, I was sick of hearing Flip laugh about how he'd made a fool of the cop. But he started again as soon as we walked into the party, telling everyone around him and laughing as loudly as he had the first time.

By now it really wasn't a lie—I really did feel sick to my stomach. He may be cute, I thought, but what an ego. This guy thinks he's in line next to Muhammad Ali.

My feeling of uneasiness grew as soon as we went into the party room. One look around told me that this wasn't the sort of place or the sort of crowd I was used to. The room had black walls and a huge palm tree in the corner. There were several big plants in hanging baskets, and they all looked as if they could be man-eating! There was no furniture except for a coffee table and some giant striped pillows. Most of the guests were still standing. They greeted Flip as we came in, and he acted like a prince visiting his people. I half expected them to kneel to him. They looked mildly interested in me, but before I could be introduced to anyone, Flip had launched into his famous police-fooling story, and I was forgotten.

As the evening wore on, I began to feel worse, not better. Flip's friends were frightening to me. They were all much older, and they really put on airs. The room was heavy with smoke, which stung my eyes and made my mascara run. None of the other girls looked like they were in high school. They were all wearing sexy outfits and looked bored while they sipped drinks.

After a while a girl approached us. She had long dark hair curling right down past her shoulders. She was wearing the tightest pink jeans, and a T-shirt with Too Hot to Handle across the front. She walked right up to Flip and slipped her arm through his.

"Hey, Flip, honey," she said, almost purring. "I'm real thirsty. How about going to find me something to drink?"

"I have a date with me, Loretta," Flip said. "This is Candy."

Loretta looked at me as if I were a cockroach and she were the man from Raid. "Oh," she said. "Where did she come from?"

"She's Freddie's sister," he answered.

"You mean Ready Freddie? He's got a sister?" she asked, starting to laugh. "She doesn't look like she's as much fun as he is."

"Give her time, Loretta—she's still young and sweet."

"So that's how you like them now, is it, Flip—young and sweet?"

I was getting pretty mad at this conversation about me going on right in front of my nose. I was beginning to feel like a piece of meat on a supermarket counter. Finally, I got up the courage to speak. "Look, if you want to discuss me, maybe I should leave. I don't enjoy standing here while you two pull me to pieces."

"It's OK, Candy," Flip said, breaking away from Loretta and laying a hand on my arm. "Come over here, and I'll get you a drink."

"Look, Flip honey," Loretta whispered loud enough for me to hear. "Come back after you've dumped Cinderella, OK?"

"You women have got to stop fighting over

118

me," Flip said. "It gives me a headache." Then he walked away.

"Well how about that!" I heard Loretta say to another girl. "What's gotten into old Flip? He's no fun anymore. It all comes of cradle-snatching."

"Well, she's very sweet," the other girl said.

"Have you ever known 'sweet' to be enough for Flip?" Loretta asked. "I bet he's just doing this to make me jealous. Well, I won't play. I'll just let Jeffrey give me a good time instead."

I stood against the wall with a man-eating plant brushing my face and wished I was anyplace but this party. Flip seemed to be taking an age to bring me that drink. I didn't like the party or the people, and I wasn't at all sure that I liked Flip. Then I saw him, a can of beer in each hand. He'd been waylaid in the middle of the room. He was standing there surrounded by admirers, and he was talking and laughing loudly between gulps of beer. I realized that what had seemed mature and fun at my school was really loudmouthed and boring. If this was being a grown-up, I didn't want any part of it.

Finally Flip moved in my direction. "Here, have a beer," he said, thrusting a can into my hand.

"Thanks, but I'll stick to Coke if you don't mind," I said.

"Come on, stop being Miss Prissy," he said, pushing the can at me.

"I really don't want to, Flip," I said. "I don't like the taste of beer, and I know my parents wouldn't want me to drink."

"Relax, will you?" he said. "What harm will one can of beer do? You've got to start growing up some time. Come on, just one can."

"I said no, Flip."

"Am I going to have to *make* you drink it?" he said, grinning and grabbing me. I realized he had already had too much to drink and that he was getting pretty aggressive. But I was not going to drink his crummy beer, however aggressive he was. I struggled free, beer splashing over both of us.

"Hey, look what you've done!" he yelled. "I just had those pants cleaned. Man—do you think I'm made of money?"

"What's wrong, Flip?" someone asked.

"This kid just wrecked my best pants," he complained.

"Take them off, Flip. I'll rinse them out for you," one girl said soothingly.

"It's your own fault, Flip. You shouldn't have brought her," Loretta said. "She doesn't belong at a grown-up party."

"You're right, I don't," I said, tears stinging my eyes. I fought them back, not wanting to cry in front of these people. "Will somebody please drive me home?"

"Where do you live, kid?" one boy asked. As it turned out, none of them wanted to drive as far as Walnut Park, and even if Flip had offered, I wouldn't have driven with him in that state. But he didn't offer. He was too busy trying to get the beer out of his pants.

"Just wait till the party's over, kid," some girl said. "Nobody wants to leave yet. We've only just gotten going here. You can sleep on Donna's bed if you want to."

"That's OK," I said, trying to sound dignified, though I could feel myself trembling. "I'll walk to my grandmother's house. She lives only a few blocks away."

I pushed past them and made for the front door. Nobody tried to stop me. I don't think anybody noticed I was gone. Especially not Flip.

I never did like walking in the dark, even when I lived in the city. I don't think I had ever been out as late as that, and I was scared stiff. But the way I felt, I'd rather be scared than stay with Flip and his horrible friends. I thought of finding a booth and calling my dad, but that would only worry my folks, and besides, I'd have to wait around somewhere for an hour in the dark. No, it was much simpler to walk to Grandma's—even if it did mean walking through all those dark streets.

The street was deserted, and I ran down it sensing a possible mugger lurking in every shadow. Shrill voices and music spilled out of windows. A cat shot in front of my feet, and my heart nearly leaped out of my chest.

By the time I reached Grandma's house, I was sweating and crying and out of breath. I hammered on her door. Nobody came. Then I began to be frightened that she wouldn't answer the door that late at night or that she had already gone to sleep and wouldn't hear me. But at last I heard the shuffle of slippered feet.

"Grandma," I called through the front door. "Grandma, open up. It's me—Candy!"

"Merciful heavens, child, what's happened to you?" she asked, seeing me as I stood on her doorstep, tears streaming down my cheeks.

"I've just learned that you were right, Grandma," I gasped. "You get your just deserts for lying."

Chapter Thirteen

In the morning when I woke up in Grandma's nice, secure bedroom, with the patchwork quilt over me and the pictures of mountain lakes on the walls, I felt like a different person. The night before I had been scared, angry, and ashamed of myself. All I felt in the morning was ready for a big breakfast—Grandma's old-fashioned breakfast complete with bacon and grits!

With breakfast inside me, I discovered that I felt something else, too—I felt free. No more pretending to the kids at school, no more making up stories about nonexistent boyfriends. Bobby V.—the motorcycle-riding, leather-jacket-wearing cool dude was no more. He and I had a big fight at a party, he had gotten drunk and behaved badly, and we had parted. Forever. I need never see him again. I could go back to being ordinary, plain old me. Also I could let Jonathan know that I was free.

The sun streamed in through the window, and the whole world felt good and full of hope. I no longer felt angry at Flip. I just felt sorry for him and his crowd. If they felt they were having fun, they were mistaken, and I was only glad that my life was not like theirs. I couldn't wait to get to school on Monday and break the news to everybody that Bobby V. was no more.

The first chance I had to see Helen was when I sat next to her in biology. Naturally I had told them all about my planned outing on Saturday. In fact, looking back on it, I suppose I even bragged about it a bit. I felt guilty and uncomfortable now about all that bragging.

"How was your date?" she whispered.

"I had a fight with Bobby V., and we broke up," I whispered back.

"You two girls in the back, kindly proceed with dissecting that worm and stop chatting," Mr. Dalton yelled. He ran his biology class as if it were the army and he were the drill sergeant.

Helen picked up a scalpel and made a half-hearted stab at the worm. I didn't even want to touch it.

"Here, you try," she said, handing me the scalpel.

"No, thanks, I'll just watch if it's all the same to you," I said, pushing the scalpel back at her. "I never did like worms."

"You can't go through a whole year's biology without cutting something up," Helen said. "Just imagine it's Bobby V., and then you won't mind hacking it to pieces."

We grinned at each other. I took the scalpel and thought about Flip. This is what you deserve, Flip, I thought and sliced the worm clean in half.

"Look what you've done, dummy," Helen whispered. She started to giggle. So did I.

"Now we both get one to practice on," I said, laughing.

"No such thing," she said in mock seriousness. "You just put it back together again."

That did it. We couldn't stop laughing until a shadow fell across our table. Mr. Dalton was standing there, and he did not look amused.

"Just what seems to be the problem, Helen?" he asked in an icy voice.

We tried hard to stop laughing, but that only made us giggle more.

"Nothing, Mr. Dalton," Helen stammered. "Candy cut this worm in half by mistake. Do you think we could have a new one?"

Some of the other kids started giggling, too.

"We do not come to biology class to ruin the specimens," Mr. Dalton said.

"I didn't mean to, Mr. Dalton," I said. "It was just a very thin worm."

Mr. Dalton looked down at us with utter disgust. "I think you had better both go outside and wait in the hall until you can act with dignity in this classroom," he said.

We left, still laughing helplessly.

"Now," Helen said as soon as we were safely outside, "you can tell me all the gory details of your fight."

"Wow," she said after I'd recounted the whole evening in detail. "What a nerd! What an ego! You are well rid of him, Candy. That dude might have been great-looking and fun, but believe me, cute is not everything! And quite frankly, that kind of guy was not right for you." She paused, then asked, "Are you going to tell Jonathan that you're through with Bobby V.?"

"I might," I answered. "If I can get up the

nerve! Unless, of course, one of my friends tells him for me."

"Well, don't look at me," she said. "I might be nice, but I'm not *that* nice. Don't forget I kind of like Jonathan myself. I might stand more chance with you out of the running."

Just then the door opened, and Mr. Dalton wanted to know if we were sorry for our bad behavior. By now we had stopped laughing, and pretty soon we were attacking a new worm.

Of course I had to see Jonathan after school for volleyball practice, but when I actually saw him, I found that telling him wasn't that easy. After all, you can't just go up to a guy you hardly know and say, "Oh, by the way, I've broken up with my boyfrend." Especially if that guy happens to be a senior and your coach. It was made even more difficult because Jonathan was in a bad mood, or more precisely, he was very keyed up.

We were playing a qualifying game the next day. If we won, we'd go to the regional tournament. Only one team per county made it to this tournament, and as number-two team in last year's league, we had the right to challenge last year's number-one team for the slot. If we lost we wouldn't go anywhere. Jonathan wanted us to win very badly. In fact, I think he wanted it more than we did. He didn't give anyone a chance to rest for a second during workout, and we had no energy left to talk about anything except volleyball. As soon as practice was over, Jonathan hurried off without a word to anyone. I watched his back and the easy swing of his walk disappear across the school yard. Will I ever get to talk to you as a human being, Jonathan? I wondered.

The next day I didn't have time to think about Jonathan, Flip, or anything other than volleyball. We were all too nervous. We didn't feel any better when the other team arrived, complete with two busloads of supporters, all talking loudly about what fun the tournament had been last year and how they couldn't wait to play again this year.

Their supporters filled our bleachers, yelling, screeching, and giggling. It was very obvious that only a handful of our kids had come to watch—mostly Diana and a few others of our crowd. Volleyball, especially girls' volleyball, wasn't a big thing at our school. We had the best football team in the area, and most of the kids only cared about that. In a way I was glad we didn't have more supporters. At least there weren't hundreds of people relying on us, expecting us to win. If we lost, we could slink away, and nobody would notice but Jonathan. I remembered, then, how very much he wanted us to win.

On my way out to the court, I bumped into a girl from their cheering section—a big, hefty blond dressed in red and white, their school colors. She even wore red shoes and red-and-white hair ribbons. As I walked by her she waved a red-and-white pom-pom in my face and shouted, "Hey, bean pole, I don't know why you guys are bothering to play at all. We're going to cream you—same as we do all the others!"

I tried to think of a witty answer to this, and I wished that Bobby V. or Helen were beside me. They were both good at snappy comebacks. But then I decided to save my breath for the game. I pushed past the girl.

We were all very nervous in warm-up. We dropped the ball and hit into the net and stumbled around.

"Come on, you guys, get with it!" Jonathan pleaded.

"We don't even need to try against this bunch of clowns," someone on the opposing team said and sneered.

The game started, and we were still much too tense, missing shots we should have scored on. A couple of times I let the ball sail past me, and Helen dove but didn't connect with it.

"What is this?" a heckler yelled from the bleachers. "A volleyball team or help the handicapped?" Laughter broke out all around her. Then we began to get mad. As we got mad we played better and better. The more dumb things the fans yelled out, the harder we played. Soon we were playing like a team again—taking risks, jumping impossibly high, not letting anything get away from us. I think the others were all feeling the same way as I was. We couldn't wait to see all those stupid faces when their team got beaten.

We did all the things Jonathan was always yelling about, and we dove for almost impossible shots. The other team was clearly surprised. They'd expected to walk all over us. By the time they woke up and saw that we were not so easy to beat, we were ahead by so much that they couldn't catch up. Their fans started screaming louder and louder until the whole gym was shaking and echoing with noise, but still they couldn't catch us. I scored a really fantastic point! I saw a high ball coming over, and as I leaped for it, I felt as if my legs had springs, almost as if I could fly. My hands touched the ball, and I brought it down hard into the backcourt.

It was strange to see the change in the fans. As soon as they saw that their team was losing, they fell silent, and some even slunk out of the gym. After the game, the other team tried to collect their things as quickly as possible, as if they were embarrassed to stick around. As I walked past two of them, I heard one girl say to the other, "Well, I wouldn't want to be like them; they're like a team of robots—at least we're sexy!"

I couldn't help smiling to myself. At that moment Jonathan came onto the court. He grabbed me, picked me up, and twirled me around like a little kid. "You did it," he said. "I'm so happy, I could kiss you."

"Why don't you, then?" I said quietly. He was still holding me tightly in his arms. Slowly he lowered my feet to the ground. I felt as if the whole air was full of electric sparks.

"Will you come and have a pizza with me tonight?" he asked.

"I'd like that," I said. Then I felt embarrassed, standing there with Jonathan's arms around me and all the world looking on. "Let me go and get showered and changed, OK?" I asked.

"I'll wait for you outside," he said, and he slowly let me go.

"I won't be long," I called over my shoulder, and, in spite of my exhausted body, I bounded toward the locker room. I sat down and undid my shoelaces as if in a dream. My heart was beating like crazy, and it wasn't from playing volleyball, either! I think the other girls spoke to me as I got undressed. I must have answered, but I really can't remember a word I said. There was only one person in the whole world who mattered right then, and, in a few moments I was going to be alone with him. I could explain everything to him. I'd make everything all right, and life would be wonderful for ever and ever.

I think I must have been psychic because I'd worn a skirt to school that day, something I hardly ever did. I was so glad that I had reached into my closet and pulled it out while I was still half asleep that morning. It was a red prairie skirt, and I wore it with a white blouse sprinkled with tiny red flowers. The outfit was a big improvement on my normal sagging, faded blue jeans and plain T-shirt. I admired myself quickly in the locker room mirror.

It was not quite dusk as I came out of the gym—the sky was just flaming, the same color as my skirt, and the whole world seemed to be rosy, as if to match my mood. Jonathan was standing alone under the big oak tree. He looked up as he heard my footsteps, and his face broke into a wonderful smile. It was so corny—like those commercials where a boy and girl run in slow motion across a meadow of high grass with their hands outstretched toward each other. But it didn't feel corny then. It felt romantic.

"Hey, you look pretty tonight," he said.

"Thanks," I mumbled.

We stood and looked awkwardly at each other.

"Shall we go?" he asked. "I've got my mother's car today. It's over in the parking lot."

As I turned to walk beside him, I heard my name called. At first I thought it couldn't be me, but then the yelling got closer.

"Hey, Candy—slow down. I've been waiting for hours!"

I looked around in disbelief. I began to think that my mind was playing tricks on me, but it was true. Flip was running down the path toward me.

"Candy, wait up," he called as he ran. "I have to talk to you!"

"Not now, Flip," I said coldly. "I'm busy."

"But I have to talk to you right now," he said. "I've been feeling so bad about the other night that I drove all the way out from the city to say I'm sorry. Can't we talk it over?"

"Look, Candy—if you'd rather—" Jonathan began.

But Flip cut in before I could. "Hey, man—butt out and just give me some time alone with my girl, will you?"

"If that's what you want," Jonathan said and turned away.

"No, Jonathan, don't go!" I called after him.

He didn't even look back as he walked away.

Chapter Fourteen

"Jonathan!" I called after him. But he seemed not to hear. He walked back into the gym, and I watched the door shut behind him.

"Let go of me," I cried hysterically and tried to struggle from Flip's grasp.

"Oh, come on, baby," Flip crooned in my ear. "Just relax, will you? You're like a little tiger! But that's how I like my girls—wild and fierce!"

"Will you get it into your thick head that I am not your girl!" I yelled at him. "I have never been your girl, and what's more I never want to be your girl, now or ever. Why don't you leave me alone and go back to those sexy ladies in the tight T-shirts at the party. They're more your type."

Flip grinned. I wondered how I could ever have found that smile wonderful. Now I just found it stupid.

"Maybe they are, baby," he said, "but a guy gets bored with the same old thing after a while. That's what I like about you—you're different from them. You're young and fresh—they've all been around. They've seen everything and done everything. That's a drag. I need some excitement back in my life."

"Well, I'm not your excitement," I said, snapping at him. "Now will you let go of me, or do I have to call the campus security guard?"

"OK, I'm going," he said. "I'll leave you to cool down. But I'll be back. Believe me, I'll be back. In fact I'll come and pick you up on Saturday. There's a good party I want to go to."

"You just don't quit, do you?" I sighed, exasperated. "I thought I made myself clear. I never want to see you again!"

"But you *will* see me again, won't you?" Flip said evenly. "Because if you don't, I'll have to tell all your little friends about your big hoax. I bet they'd love to find out how you made jackasses of them all—they'd love to know that Bobby V. never even existed."

"You wouldn't do that," I said shakily. "Why, that's nothing but blackmail."

He grinned again. "That's right. Just like you used on Freddie and me to get me to come to the dance with you."

I had an urge to slap that grinning face. "Well, go ahead, see if anyone cares when you tell them," I said, though I wasn't feeling as brave as I sounded. I felt as if I were in an elevator plunging faster and faster into a bottomless shaft and I didn't know how to stop it. I broke away from Flip.

"Now, get out of here," I said. "Tell the whole world for all I care but just stay away from me!"

"All right, I'm going," he said. "But I have a feeling I'll be back. See ya, baby." Then he strolled away as if he hadn't a care in the world.

I stood there alone in the twilight. A cold wind whipped at my prairie skirt. I shivered and kept looking toward that gym door. Did I dare go after Jonathan and explain to him? Would Jonathan even listen to me—after all, he was not famous for his great temper at the best of times, and this sure was not the best of times! Was he even still there? Perhaps he'd slipped out through the other door and had already gone home . . . perhaps . . . perhaps . . . perhaps . . .

I knew that I had to go. If I wanted Jonathan, it was now or never. I made my feet walk down the path. I made my fingers pull open the door.

At first I thought he had gone. My footsteps echoed across the empty gym. Then I saw him, sitting on the top step of the bleachers, his chin resting in his hands, just staring out into the darkness.

"Jonathan?"

"What do you want?" he murmured.

"Why did you leave? I begged you not to."

He didn't look at me but went on staring out over my head. "I make it my policy never to interfere between boyfriend and girlfriend."

"Jonathan," I pleaded, "he's not my boyfriend."

"No? Well, he does a pretty good imitation of it," he said bitterly. He stood up, picked up his sports bag, and started to walk down the steps toward me. "What was that he said? Butt out and leave me alone with my girl—something like that."

"You don't understand," I begged. "It's not like that at all."

"You're right, I don't understand," he said. He walked straight past me, almost as though I weren't there, and on toward the door.

"Jonathan—please wait," I begged. "Won't

138

you please just listen to me? I have to explain some things to you—please, Jonathan?"

"You don't have to explain anything to me, Candy," he said, turning back to look at me. "I mean nothing to you."

"But you do, Jonathan," I blurted out.

There was a moment's silence. Jonathan stood there like a figure carved out of ebony.

"I do?" he asked huskily.

I nodded, feeling shy, yet relieved.

"Then what about that guy?" he asked.

"That's what I've been trying to tell you," I said. "I told a stupid lie when I first came to this school that I had a fantastic boyfriend in the city. It was one of the dumbest things I've ever done because then they wanted to meet him, so I had to sort of borrow my brother's friend. That's who that boy was—Freddie's friend. I thought it was only for one evening and I could forget the whole thing, but I made a mistake. The trouble is that he likes me, and he hasn't quit pestering me ever since. I've just told him to get lost forever. I hope it's sunk in this time."

There was another silence. "So you see," I continued uneasily, "there never was a boy-friend. . . . Only now you can see that I'm not a very nice sort of person—I tell lies, and my grandmother always said that liars come to a bad end. So perhaps you won't want me now, anyway. . . ."

Jonathan had put down his book bag and turned back toward me. I looked at his face, my eyes pleading, begging him to understand. Then I saw his mouth twitch at the corners in a smile.

"That's what your grandma said, is it?" he asked.

I nodded.

"You know what I think?" he asked. The smile spread across his face. "I think you've probably been punished enough. I can't think of a worse punishment than having to spend a whole evening with Mr. Macho there!"

"Oh, Jonathan," I said, "if you only knew—"

I took a step toward him, and he took a step toward me. Then his arms reached out toward me, and he was holding me and kissing me.

It was not like Flip's kiss, not quite so smooth and expert, perhaps—he probably hadn't had as much practice. First he took my shoulders firmly in those big hands and drew me toward him. Then his lips brushed mine, almost hesitantly, as if he weren't quite sure of either of us. Then he looked down at me, gazing into my eyes as if waiting for the go-ahead to kiss me properly. I looked back at him, and I could almost feel the electricity flowing between our eyes.

Suddenly he hugged me. It was so different from the way Flip had made me feel. With Flip I had soared up to the moon, but this felt warm and wonderful, like returning home. I knew definitely and positively that no one since Adam and Eve had ever felt that way before.

Chapter Fifteen

After I called my folks, we drove toward the pizza restaurant in silence. Jonathan had one hand on the steering wheel and the other lay beside him in mine. I was in a daze as if it couldn't really be happening to me. It was as if everything I had felt until then—the way I had longed for Flip to telephone, the excitement I felt at my first dance—had just been a practice for Jonathan. For now I had found the real thing, there was no mistaking it.

I wondered why I hadn't admitted to myself on the very first day that Jonathan was the only boy I wanted. Even if he had yelled at me and made me work unbearably hard, I had known deep down that he was the one.

We reached the pizza parlor. Music from the jukebox and soft, warm light spilled out from the big windows and open door. A group of kids from school was hanging around outside, laughing and filling up on pizza.

"Hi, Jon," one of them called when he saw us. "We're just about to get a second pie. Want to join us?"

"Er—no thanks, guys, not right now," Jonathan said, squeezing my hand.

"Why don't you wake up, man," another boy interrupted. "Can't you see he has a date with him?"

We walked past them into the restaurant. It was lit by the reddish glow of tinted light bulbs. The music was so loud that you could feel it in the soles of your feet.

Jonathan drew me close to him. "Hey, Candy," he whispered, "would you mind very much if we just got a pizza to go and drove somewhere? This place is too public. I don't want to be part of the crowd right now."

It was funny how we both shared the same feelings—that was just what I'd been thinking, too.

We ordered the pizza, which seemed to take forever to bake, while almost everyone we knew from school came in.

"Hi, Jonathan, hi, Candy," they said. Some of them gave us knowing looks as if they had suspected something like this would happen between us. I began to feel so self-conscious that I was ready to hide in the ladies' room until the order was ready. But Jonathan was feeling the same way. "What is this—reunion night?" he said. "I've never seen so many kids here."

That's right, I thought. I've nothing to feel self-conscious about. I have a wonderful boy here with me. So what. Let them look.

That shows what a long way I had come in a couple of months. At Lincoln High I would have died if all those people had stared at me.

Ginger came in too, and when she saw us, she gave me a huge grin. "Well," she said, "I see all the best people in town meet here! I can't stop—Mom's out of town, and Dad doesn't trust my cooking, thank heavens!" She went up to the counter, grabbed the pizza that was waiting for her, and hurried out. But as she passed, she looked back at me and winked.

At long last our pizza was ready. "I was beginning to think they personally went to the ocean to catch the anchovies," Jonathan whispered as we walked up to collect it.

"Or to Canada for the Canadian bacon!" I quipped back.

"Or to Italy for the salami!"

We were giggling like little kids as we walked

back to the car. As we drove out of town, the street lights became fewer and fewer, and the pools of darkness bigger and blacker.

"Where are we going?" I asked at last.

"We're going to have a picnic," Jonathan said seriously. "And the best place for a picnic around here is on Blue Ridge. Don't tell me you've never been on Blue Ridge before?"

"Well, I haven't. We've only been here a few months, remember?"

I thought about it as I said it. We had only been there a few months. It was amazing what had happened in that time.

The road snaked up and up the mountain, and Jonathan needed two hands on the wheel to drive around the bends. I was busy steadying the pizza, trying to stop it from sliding off the seat. Jonathan finally turned off the road, and the car bumped along a dirt track.

"Here we are," Jonathan said and switched off the engine. We opened the doors and climbed out. The silence was fantastic—just a gentle sigh of night wind in the grass, and a few crickets chirping far away; otherwise, it was total silence. The stars looked so close that you almost felt you could reach out and touch them. We might have been in another world. Way down below, the lights of Walnut Park twinkled like those of a magic land.

"Jonathan, it's beautiful!" I said.

"Is it?" he asked. "I hadn't really noticed." His arms came around me again, and he kissed me one long, beautiful kiss after another.

After a while I pulled away. "I hate to be unromantic," I said, "especially at a time like this. But I'm starving, and if we let that pizza get any colder, it won't taste at all nice."

Jonathan laughed. "What a girl," he said. "Only thinks of her stomach when she could be in the arms of the sexiest guy in Walnut Park."

"I bet you're hungry, too," I said. "Go on, admit it."

"All right, I admit it," he said. "I am starving. Let's eat!"

So we sat on a patch of grass in the dark and shared a pizza. We discovered all sorts of little things we had in common—that we both liked mushrooms and hated green pepper and liked anchovies, sometimes, and in small amounts.

"You know," Jonathan said, looking at me and shaking his head, "I knew from the first moment I saw you that we were right for each other."

"You sure didn't show it," I said. "You yelled at me and made me dive onto that hard floor until every bone in my body was broken."

He smiled. "You can blame that on Jonathan Robbins, the coach, not the person," he said. "But I do admit that I was kind of hard on you. In fact, I was pretty mean, now that I look back on it. But I couldn't help it. You see, as soon as I saw you, I knew how I felt about you, and I wanted to ask you out. But I'd heard that you already had a steady boy, so I tried not to give away how I was feeling."

"So you acted extra mean to make up for it," I said.

He nodded. "Something like that."

We ate our pizza in silence until I said, "Jonathan, why didn't you tell me how you felt about me sooner?"

"I guess I didn't want to make a fool of myself," he said slowly. "You see, there was this girl last year. I thought she liked me, but she let me down pretty bad. I didn't want to go through all that again."

I reached across and took his hand.

"My problem is, I suppose," he said slowly, "that I'm too shy. I don't feel sure of myself, and I don't know how to act, especially around girls."

"Oh, come on," I said, laughing. "That's a bunch of baloney. Look how you bully a whole volleyball team."

"Well, that's different," he said. "I know I'm

a good volleyball coach. I know what I'm talking about. When I'm the coach and you're the players, I feel OK about myself. But when I have to talk to a girl, I get all nervous and clam up."

"I haven't noticed you being shy and nervous around me," I said teasingly.

"That's because you're special," he said. "I saw that the first time we met. I looked at you, standing there looking at me with those big eyes, and I thought—she looks scared and shy, too. I bet she'd understand how it feels!"

I looked out over the town. My heart felt too full to speak. Down below a car detached itself from the shimmer of lights and began to climb upward—two little lights going back and forth across the blackness of the mountain. How strange life is, I thought. Who would ever have believed that Jonathan was shy? He seemed like he had the whole world at his fingertips, and nobody knew except me that he had those outbursts of temper only because he didn't feel sure of himself.

"Now that we have each other, Jonathan," I said, giving him a little smile, "we can both be shy together!"

Chapter Sixteen

When I was a little kid, I sometimes prayed that I would never grow up. I was scared of having to live in a world where you could never cry or show your feelings, scared of never being able to act scared. That's the way I thought grown-ups were—perfect, and never shy or scared.

Then I remember the time I saw my mother cry. My brother had been hit by a car and knocked off his bike. While we waited in that cold, tiled hospital waiting room to find out how badly he was hurt, my mother cried. My dad was pretty close to crying, too. That was the first time I realized that perhaps grown-ups were not quite as grown up as I had thought.

I grew up a bit myself, that evening with

Jonathan. I had always thought that I was the only dummy who was still scared of things, and that seniors, especially senior boys, were strong and powerful and very mature. It made me feel a lot better about myself to realize that I was not alone. I felt so wonderful, I just had to tell somebody. I got up very early and wrote it all down for Bobby V.

"I don't think you would know me now," I finished. "In fact the old, shy, klutzy Candy Davis is no more. Not only do I have a fantastic (and let me repeat FANTASTIC, not to mention SUPER, GORGEOUS, INCREDIBLE, TOTALLY AWESOME) boyfriend, but I am also one of the top players in the volleyball team that has made it to a big tournament at Hillside High next week. So if you want to see a real superstar in action, you had better come and watch me play."

The next day I had another eye-opener about senior boys—to be more exact, about that mature man-about-town, my brother Freddie. It made me realize that we were all the same, really—little kids and teenagers and parents and old people—that we all needed the same things, love and security and someone to care for us.

Freddie arrived home unexpectedly on Friday evening right in the middle of dinner. He usually waited until Saturday morning to come home.

"Well, that boy has a talent for smelling food a mile away," my mother said, beaming with pleasure as he walked in. "Trust you to show up in time for a meal!"

"To what do we owe this honor?" Dad asked, teasing. "Run out of clean shirts before a date?"

Then my mother noticed Freddie's face. "What's wrong, son?" she asked. "Is something the matter?"

"I had a fight with the Joneses," he said. "They told me they didn't want me staying there anymore."

"Oh, Freddie," my mother said, looking hurt. "What did you do?"

"It wasn't one thing," Freddie said, sitting down at the table and reaching for a plate. "It was a lot of little things." He looked away from my mother, exactly the way he used to when he'd been caught raiding the cookie jar. "Like I played the stereo too loud at night or I forgot to put the milk back in the fridge. Gosh, Mom, you've no idea how fussy they were. If I put my glass down on a table without a coaster, they yelled. Or if I sat on a pillow or dropped a crumb, they were always going on and on about it. They treat their own son the same way. He spends all his life creeping around as if he's scared of getting yelled at. That's no way to live, is it?"

"Well, I suppose you'll have to come home and finish up school here," my dad said, looking worried.

"That would be too hard on the boy," my mother interrupted. She turned to Freddie. "I'll see if Mother can take you in. It's only for a couple of months, and I wouldn't want your grades to suffer."

Freddie's face broke into a big, happy, little-boy smile. "I wouldn't mind going to Gran's," he said. "She's all right. She knows how to cook, too."

"Didn't they feed you properly?" my mother asked. "I thought you were looking a bit underfed."

"You should have seen it," Freddie said, piling a huge helping of potatoes onto his plate. "Macaroni and cheese, every night the same. I'll throw up if I ever see macaroni and cheese again."

For a while he ate in silence.

"By the way, Freddie," my mother said, "have you seen any more of that nice boy, Flip?"

I looked down very hard at my plate and pretended to be cutting up a piece of meat.

"Him!" Freddie grunted.

"I thought he was such a nice, polite boy," my mother said.

"Shows how you can be wrong about people," Freddie said. "He borrowed ten dollars from me, and now he won't pay it back. He says he doesn't remember borrowing it at all."

"Well, who would have thought it?" my mother said. "He seemed very polite. Candy was kind of sweet on him for a while—weren't you, Candy?"

I had spared my parents the details of the party disaster. I didn't want to lie to them—I had gotten into enough trouble doing that—so when I had called from Grandma's, I just said that it had gotten late, and I had decided to stay over at her house.

"For a while," I said, not looking up.

"So I hear," Freddie said, looking at me questioningly. "But I'd drop him if I were you, Candy. He's not the kind of guy you can trust. Believe me."

"Don't worry. I believe," I said. "I *have* dropped him."

"No kidding?" he asked. "From what he said, I thought you two were still going together. Something about a party this Saturday?"

"No way!" I exploded.

"That's good," he said. "Because I want better for you than that."

He looked around the table and beamed at us all. "Hey, it's *good* to be home. I can't tell you all how much I missed you—even you, little sister. It can be real lonely in the city!"

Well, what do you know?

Chapter Seventeen

"Do you realize," Helen asked us as she turned over on her back to look at the blue sky, "that only three days from now we'll be playing in the big tournament?"

It was one of those rare spring days when the sky is like a blue glass bowl and all the earth is glowing with new colors. The breeze was warm and gentle, whispering the promise of summer. All the kids were sitting together at lunch on the grass beside the football field, and until then we hadn't spoken much, just soaked up the new sunshine. Helen brought us back to reality.

"Must you remind us of unpleasant things like that?" Sharron asked. "I was just drifting off to sleep!"

"I don't know why we bother to go," Cindy

155

murmured. "We don't stand a chance of winning. The whole thing is a waste of time."

"That's defeatist talk. We'll have to report you to Jonathan at once," Helen said, trying to sound fierce.

"Oh, yes, I keep forgetting that we have a spy in our midst now," Crissy said. "Anything we say gets carried straight back to the great dictator immediately!"

I grinned. "So you'd better watch out, hadn't you?" I said lazily. I didn't even mind the kidding around anymore. It was good to be part of it—not an outsider they were just polite to. And I knew they were really glad about Jonathan and me. It meant we were another twosome—we fitted right in.

"I must say," Diana said, stretching languidly in the warm grass, "a change for the better has come over old Jonathan since you took him over, Candy."

"I agree," Sharron added. "He's not nearly so crabby at workouts now."

"And he barely ever yells," Helen said. "Or at least not quite so loudly."

"He doesn't yell at *Candy* at all!" Crissy teased. "It's always—'Listen, honeybunch, would you mind throwing your cute little body at that ball just a wee bitty quicker?' "

"That's not true, and you know it," I said,

laughing. "He yells at me just as much as at the rest of you. Whatever he may think about me in private, when we're on that court, I'm just another volleyball player like everyone else."

"Oh, sure," Helen said, teasing. "But then most volleyball coaches go around kissing their players all the time."

"Hey, knock it off, you guys," I said. "Anyone would think I was the only person around here with a boyfriend. I don't tease you about George."

"There's nothing to tease about, honey," Helen said and sighed. "Because there's nothing vaguely amusing about him. In fact, George is just a big old bore who hardly notices I'm around."

"I heard that, and I resent it," came the muffled words from George's sleeping body.

"Oh, you hush up and go back to sleep, this is girl talk," Helen said, giving him a poke with her foot.

We all laughed.

"Don't worry, Candy," Crissy said. "We're only teasing you because it's new and because it's such a strange experience for us to see crabby old Jonathan in love."

"Speak of the devil," Helen muttered.

We all looked up. Jonathan had seen us

and was walking across the grass toward where we were sitting.

"You're just in time, we nearly finished all the food," Helen called to him. "Want a sandwich? I think it's tuna—if George hasn't rolled on it yet."

Jonathan smiled, something he did a lot more often now. "No, thanks. I just came to get Candy."

"As if we couldn't guess why you came," Helen said. "Unless it was to drag all us poor girls to extra practice for your dumb tournament."

"Now that's a good idea," Jonathan said. "We'll have an hour's practice at lunchtime as well as after school!"

"You and your big mouth, Helen," Sharron said.

"He's only joking," I said quickly. Then I turned to him anxiously. "You are only joking, aren't you?"

"For the others, yes," he said, reaching down a hand to me and pulling me to my feet. "I think you need some extra help with your game, so I plan to give you a lot of private, special coaching!" He put an arm round my shoulder as we walked away, and I felt, as I had felt a million times during the last week

158

or so, This can't be happening to me. Someone will pinch me, and I'll wake up!

But I didn't wake up. The wonderful dream kept right on going until I was actually riding in the bus to the tournament with Jonathan beside me. Other girls were bundles of nerves, talking in short, jittery sentences or giggling like grade-schoolers. I couldn't even feel nervous. What is one volleyball tournament compared to having Jonathan as a boyfriend? I thought. I'm going to play my very best today, just for him! Because I know how much he wants to win. But even if we lose, it's only a game—it really doesn't matter. Not like being in love really matters.

As the countryside flashed past, I closed my eyes and let my imagination wander through a future with Jonathan—Jonathan and me going to picnics in the summer, going to the Senior Ball, maybe, and staying out all night. . . .There was so much to look forward to, everything had worked out beautifully. There was nothing to stand in my way forevermore.

"You guys go and get changed, then meet me on the court in ten minutes for warm-up," Jonathan said as we walked into the school where they were holding the tournament. It was a typical city high school, just like my old one—a big, dirty brick building with bars at the windows and litter piled in drifts in the school yard. I remembered how a few months ago I'd begged to be allowed to stay. But then a few months ago I could never have guessed that shy, scared bean pole Candy Davis would have come out of her shell so fast. I was now a good-looking girl who had friends, a fantastic boyfriend, and had turned into a *mean* volleyball player. It was all too incredible to believe.

We walked down the dingy, tiled hallways toward the locker rooms. As we opened the door, a roar of voices greeted us. Obviously we were one of the last teams to arrive, and every inch of space seemed to be filled with chatting, shrieking, giggling, yelling girls. We found ourselves a few inches in a corner and tried to get changed. Changing was like a magic trick in itself—pulling off clothes in the midst of hundreds of bodies.

I was sitting on the bench trying to do up a shoe when I heard a voice yelling above the others, "Are you the team from Walnut Park?"

"Right on," someone answered back.

"See, I told you it was them," the voice yelled. "Do you have a kid called Candy playing for you?"

I looked up curiously, but all I could see were my teammates' backs.

"Yeah—she's back here somewhere," they said. "Hey, Candy, get over here!"

I started to stand up, one shoe still in my hand.

"Who wants me?" I asked.

"Tell her she has an old friend wants to see her—someone who used to know her at Lincoln—Bobby V. Pearson!"

Then the crowd parted, and there was Bobby V., grinning at me delightedly. "Hey, Candy, surprise!!" she yelled. "You said I ought to come watch you play, so I tagged along with the team from Lincoln. They're in this tournament, too, you know. I can't wait to find out what a superjock you've turned into." She turned to Helen and Crissy who were nearest her. "We used to be best friends back in the city. We've kept in touch by letters. Did she ever tell you about me?"

"She sure did," Helen said slowly. "So you're Bobby V., eh?"

I felt the room spinning around me. I didn't wait to hear any more. I fought like a mad thing to push my way through the crowd. Then I ran for all I was worth. Ran and ran, down those empty clattering halls, trying to escape from their terrible laughter.

Chapter Eighteen

It seemed like hours later when I felt a hand on my shoulder. I was huddled in a dark corner next to a janitor's closet—a corner that smelled of floor polish and disinfectant and stale orange peels. I had cried until there were no more tears left to cry. I turned my tear-stained face up, and there were Jonathan's beautiful brown eyes.

"Just what do you think you're doing here?" he demanded. He sounded angry as he turned me toward him. "Do you know that we have been searching every inch of this entire building looking for you? Do you know that our team is scheduled to play"—he looked at his watch—"three and a half minutes from now?"

"Jonathan, I can't go back there, ever," I murmured. "Something terrible happened—

the worst thing possible. I told you that I made up a boyfriend called Bobby V.; well, the real Bobby V. showed up—so now they all know that she's a girl, and that I never had a boyfriend at all. They know I'm a liar and a loser, and they won't ever want to be friends with me again."

I had expected him to understand, to put his arms around me and comfort me. Instead he tried to drag me to my feet.

"Look, Candy, can you imagine what they'll think about you if you don't show up to play? The team will have to scratch—do you want that on your conscience?" Then he looked at me, and his voice softened, "Come on, get up and dry those eyes. You're making far too big a thing of this."

"Too big a thing? Those girls'll laugh at me, if they want anything to do with me at all." I started to sob again. "I thought you'd be on my side, but you're yelling at me, too."

Jonathan reached out and drew me close to him. "Look, Candy," he said softly. "Right now I have to be your coach, and I have a whole team to think of. They're all worried sick because you've run off and they can't find you. They're waiting to play, they want to play—don't you owe that to them?"

"But I *can't* go back!" I wailed in a shaky voice. "I just can't face them—I know I can't."

"You can't run away from things all your life, Candy," Jonathan said gently. "You're a big girl now. You have to face up to things, even if you don't like them. And you have to start believing in yourself. When you first started playing volleyball, you didn't believe you'd be any good, did you?"

I nodded but couldn't say anything.

"Well, I believed you'd be good, so I had to yell at you until you saw that you could be good. Now you have to believe that the other girls like you for yourself, not for some imaginary boyfriend. Do you think other people don't do dumb things to get themselves accepted and liked? They understand that. They may have laughed for a minute—after all, it was a big shock for them, and pretty funny, too, when you think of it. But if you're a nice person and they're nice people, they'll go on being your friends. And you *are* a nice person, I can swear to that!"

"But how can I face them? What will they say?" I stammered.

"Believe me, right now they are only concerned with getting you back on that court and winning the game," he said. "Now come on before it's too late." He took my hand and dragged me down the hall.

Just before we reached the gym, he stopped and looked at me tenderly. "You're a dummy, you know?" he said. "I didn't laugh when you told me, did I? And I didn't stop liking you, did I? You have to trust your friends too. Now come here and give me a kiss—then run like crazy, or we'll be disqualified."

Jonathan was right. No one laughed as I came onto the court. No one said anything about my red eyes. The other team was waiting on the other side of the net. They looked at me with interest and probably thought that I had cracked under the strain of playing in a big tournament.

I took my place in the starting lineup.

"Thank heavens you got here," Helen said. "We've been so worried. Crissy wanted to call the police."

"We couldn't find you anywhere," Sharron added. "Are you OK?"

I nodded.

One by one they each said something reassuring to me. Nobody even mentioned Bobby V. As soon as we started the game, I realized that I hadn't had a chance to warm up and that my teammates had been looking for me instead of warming up, too. My whole body felt stiff and awkward as if there was no life in my fingers and toes. I knew I was playing badly. I fumbled easy balls, and I didn't move quickly enough. When I tried to jump for the high ones, I felt like I had lead shoes on.

Luckily for us, the other team played badly, too. They were obviously nervous and missed lots of easy shots, so we won, but only just.

As soon as we came off the court, Jonathan grabbed me. "Come on, Candy, you can do better than that," he said. "Remember you belong to a team. You've got to forget about yourself. And if you feel bad, now's the time to make it up to those girls. Make them glad you're on their team!" He pulled me closer to him. "And make me proud of you, too, OK?" he whispered. Then he released me and said in a strong voice, "Now get out there and show them your stuff, girl! We've got to win the rest of the games, too!" He pushed me back onto the court with a loud slap on my behind.

After that everything felt better. I gradually regained my confidence as my body warmed up. I started leaping well and moving fast. We kept on winning. Until the last game of all. By a strange coincidence we found ourselves in the finals playing against the team from my old school, Lincoln; and they were really tough. I was trying so hard by now that I hardly noticed the faces of old acquaintances on the other side of the net. I was trying harder than I had ever tried before. But it was no good. However high I jumped, however hard I spiked, the ball came sailing back over the net as if it were on a piece of elastic.

They were just too good for us. Each time we changed server, I would pass a teammate drenched in sweat, like me, gasping for breath, like me. I didn't notice much gasping coming from the other side of the net. They all looked fresh and ready for action.

We had already played four rounds to reach the finals, and I bet we had to struggle harder to get there than the Lincoln team. At that point we were totally and utterly pooped. At least I was. I tried to command my arms to move and my legs to bounce, but they just wouldn't obey. Even Jonathan wasn't yelling anymore.

Then the final whistle came. At that time we were so exhausted that I don't think any of us cared who won or lost. We shook hands with the winners. I was filled with a deep sense of failure. I saw Helen standing beside me, and I remembered how nice she and all the others had been about me running away. Perhaps if I hadn't run away, I would have had more energy. Perhaps they would have had more energy if they hadn't had to worry and look for me.

"Look, I'm sorry," I mumbled. "I let you all down. I'm sorry."

Then I walked into the locker room. I was pulling off my shoes when Helen came and sat beside me.

"Will you stop laying the blame for everything on yourself?" she said. "You are one big walking guilt trip! You didn't let anybody down. We lost. They're better than we are, and we lost. It's as simple as that. If you were Superwoman, we still would have lost to that team, and you know it."

"I don't know it at all," I said. "If I hadn't made such a fool of myself before—"

Helen touched my arm. "Candy," she said gently, "do you think we only judge you as a friend by the way you play volleyball or the sort of boyfriend you have? You don't have to perform for me to be my friend. You just have to be yourself. I like you for yourself, and so do the others. Do you understand that?"

I tried a watery smile. "Thanks, Helen," I said.

"Now for heaven's sake, go and talk to that Bobby V. character," Helen said, giving me a shove. "She's been hanging around all day waiting for a chance to see you."

I walked over to the other side of the locker room where the Lincoln team was celebrating noisily.

"Hey, Candy," Bobby V. called. "Come over here and meet the team. Guys, this is my good old buddy Candy Davis. She used to be at Lincoln, too."

"How come you never went out for the team there?" a tall redhead asked.

"I'd never even played until I got to Walnut Park," I said.

"That's too bad. We could have used you, you're a good player."

"Yeah, you guys gave us our best game all day," someone else added.

I tried a gracious smile. "We did our best," I said, "but you were just too good."

"Don't we know it," the redhead said. "We're the greatest!"

"And so modest, too," her teammate butted in.

Bobby V. left the Lincoln team and took my arm. "Hey, Candy, I didn't get a chance to talk to you before," she said. "Did you have bad news or something? I saw you go rushing off in a hurry."

"You mean the other girls didn't tell you what was wrong?"

"They didn't say anything. They were all rushing around trying to find you again. What was wrong, anyway?"

"It's OK. It's all taken care of now," I said. "Everything is fine again."

"That's good," she said, giving me her big smile. "Hey, you *have* changed. I'd hardly recognize you. You look much more grown up. And you don't look so scared anymore. You used to look like you'd run and hide if anyone said 'boo' to you. She laughed. "And who would have thought that you'd make a superjock? What made you change like that?"

"I found someone who believed in me," I said. "He thought I could do it long before I thought I could."

"So it was the wonderful, fantastic, incredible boyfriend who's responsible for the new Candy Davis?" she said. "I can't wait to meet him. By the way, I never got around to asking you, whatever happened to that boy you made up?"

"It's all over and forgotten," I said, smiling a little. "It worked out all right."

"Well, thank heavens for that," she said. "That sort of thing could have gotten you into a real mess. After all, you aren't as cool as me! Listen, you want to go and have a soda somewhere and talk?"

"I'd like to," I said, "but I already promised my team we'd go for a pizza. Why don't you come with us?"

"If you don't think I'd be in the way," she said, hesitating a little and showing me that she, too, had changed. The old Bobby V. would never have hesitated for anything.

"Of course you won't be in the way," I said. "You're my best friend, remember? I want you to meet a really great bunch of kids, not to mention one super fantastic guy."

"Candy, come on, I'm starving," one of our team called. "And Jonathan's waiting!" I took Bobby V. by the arm, and we all left the building, talking noisily. Suddenly I bumped into the last person in the world I had expected to see.

"Flip—what on earth are you doing here?" I said angrily.

"Hiya, baby. Freddie told me you'd be here," he said smoothly. "So I came to collect you. There's a party tonight I want to take you to. See, I'm wearing wash-and-wear jeans tonight. Not taking any chances!"

"You must be very slow on the uptake," I said patiently. "I've told you I'm not going anywhere with you ever again! Hasn't that sunk in yet? Besides, I already have a date, thank you."

"Suit yourself," Flip said smoothly. "Only I shall just have to tell all these people the details of our little relationship, and that might be a bit embarrassing for you." He grinned the whole while, his smooth, oily grin.

Then Jonathan stepped forward. He towered over Flip. "What exactly did you want to tell us, man?" he asked. "That you acted the part of her boyfriend once? Big deal! We'll send you an Oscar for it! We all know. That's old news around here. So why don't you get lost—the lady does not want to see you again." He put his arm around my shoulder. "Come on, Candy, let's go get that pizza," he said.

And we walked past Flip, standing there like a statue with his mouth open.